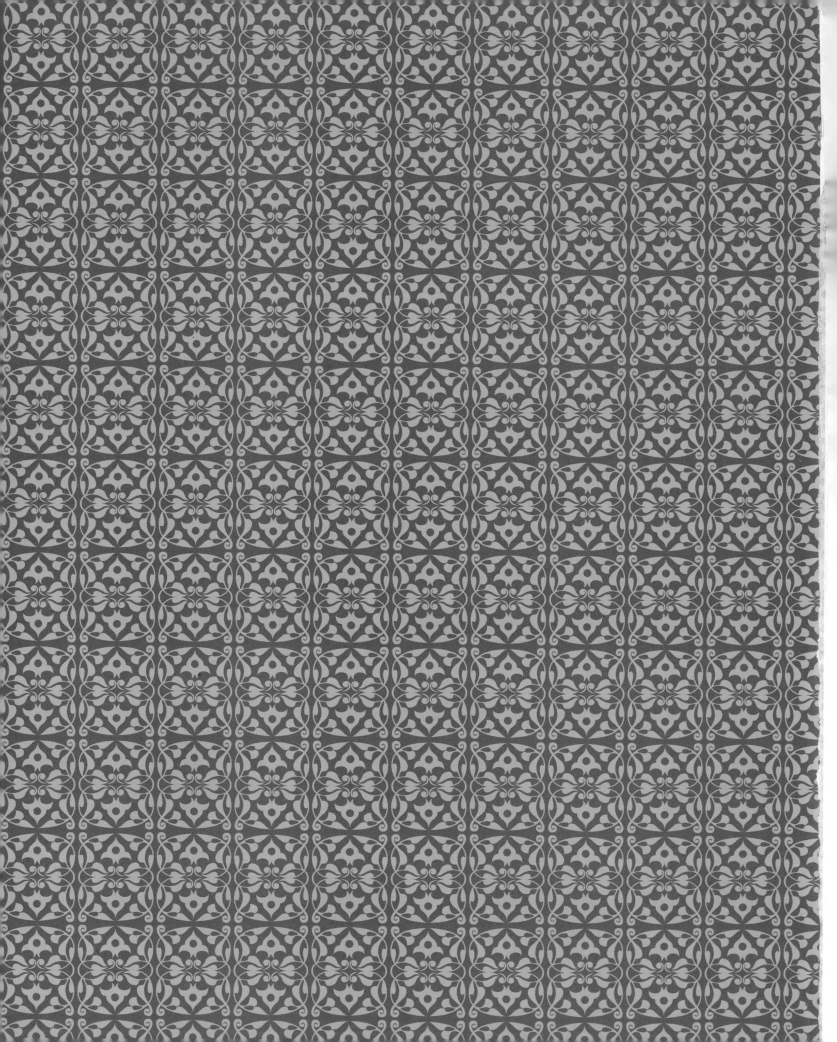

C L A S S I C
BEDTIME
STORIES

PUBLICATIONS INTERNATIONAL, LTD.

Cover illustrated by Michael Jaroszko
Title page illustrated by David Grasso

Louis Weber, C.E.O.
Publications International, Ltd.
7373 North Cicero Avenue
Lincolnwood, Illinois 60712

Once upon a time...

CONTENTS

The Frog Prince

Adapted by Eric Fein
Illustrated by Kathy Mitchell

Once upon a time, in a kingdom far away, there lived a king who had many beautiful children. But the most beautiful was his youngest daughter.

In the summer, when the kingdom broiled with heat, the young princess would sit by the edge of a deep, cool well and daydream. And sometimes, she would play with her favorite golden ball. She would toss the ball high into the air and catch it.

One afternoon, as she was playing with her golden ball, she threw it up into the air a little too high. She ran after it. But before she could catch it, it fell into the well.

The well was much too deep for the princess to get her ball. Were she to climb in, she would not be able to climb back out. The only thing she could do was lean over the side, look into the well, and weep over the loss of her beautiful golden ball.

"What will I do without my lovely golden ball?" she cried. "Won't somebody help me?"

She wept for quite some time, until she heard a voice say, "What troubles you, fair young princess?"

The princess looked down into the well and saw a frog sitting amongst the cattails.

"I am crying because my golden ball is lost in the well," the princess told the frog.

The frog said, "Weep no more, fair princess, for I shall rescue your golden ball. Though I must know, what shall you give me for performing such a deed?"

"Oh, anything you desire," she said.

"Promise that you will love me and have me as your friend, that you will take me home and share your food with me, and that at night, you will tuck me into bed with you," said the frog.

"Oh, yes, dear frog. I agree to what you ask," said the princess, but she was lying.

Overjoyed that the princess agreed to his terms, the frog dove under the water and found the golden ball. It was stuck tightly in the mud and he had to work hard to free it.

As soon as the frog set the ball down, the princess snatched it up and took off running.

The poor frog could not keep up with the princess. He called after her, "Wait, princess, wait! You didn't take me! Come back!"

But the princess was halfway home.

That evening, the royal family was enjoying their dinner when there came a shout, "Young princess, let me in!"

The princess turned pale. She excused herself from the table and opened the door to let the frog inside.

The frog looked around and said, "My, what a nice home you have. I will enjoy living here." He sniffed the air and said, "Is that beef stew I smell?" Then the frog jumped onto the table.

The king said, "Daughter, will you please tell me why there is a frog at the dinner table?"

The princess explained about how the ball fell into the well and how she had made a promise to the frog for the ball's return.

The king told the princess that she must keep her promise.

Sadly, the princess turned to the frog and said, "My dinner is your dinner. My friendship is for you, and my bed is your bed."

"Wonderful," croaked the frog as he began to eat all the food on her plate. His tongue lashed out over and over to grab the food. He had two helpings of everything. The princess lost her appetite watching the frog eat.

"Now I am tired," said the frog. "Take me to your room. The first thing I want to see in the morning is your beautiful face."

The princess began to weep, "I cannot go through with this. It is too horrible. I refuse."

"No more weeping. I am tired, take me to bed," said the frog.

The frog's teasing was too much for the princess. "No, I won't, you horrible frog." She slammed her palm on the table. The table shook and the frog lost his balance. He fell off the table.

Suddenly, the frog turned into a handsome young prince.

"What is going on here?" asked the princess.

The prince explained, "Dear princess, I am so sorry to have caused you so much pain, but an evil witch turned me into a frog. The only way I could become a prince again was to get a princess angry at me. Since princesses hardly ever lose their temper, I thought I was doomed to live the rest of my life as a frog. Then you appeared with your golden ball, and I saw you lose it. I thought it was my only chance to break the spell."

"You poor thing," said the princess. "Such a handsome young man, destined for the lonely life of a frog. How horrible!"

In that brief moment, the princess and the prince fell in love. The princess forgave the prince for deceiving her and making her mad. She was taken by the honesty in his voice.

The prince proposed marriage to the princess, and the princess accepted. The prince and the princess lived a long and happy life together.

The princess still plays with her golden ball, but now she has someone to catch it. It will never end up in the well again.

The Tortoise and the Hare

Adapted by Carolyn Quattrocki
Illustrated by Tim Ellis

Once upon a time, in a great forest, there lived a hare and a tortoise. Tortoise was slow with everything he did. He sometimes ate his breakfast so slowly that it was almost time for lunch before he had finished. He kept his house clean and neat, but he did it at his own pace—very slowly.

Hare, on the other hand, was quick as a wink in all that he did. He would be up in the morning, finished with his breakfast, and going for an early walk in the forest before Tortoise had gotten out of bed. Hare could not imagine how Tortoise could stand to be so slow all the time.

Tortoise lived next door to his good friend, Squirrel. Squirrel had a cozy little home high up in an old oak tree. She loved to spend her time scurrying around. She thought it was fun to jump from branch to branch. Squirrel, like Hare, wondered how Tortoise could always be so slow.

Hare lived near his old friend, Owl, who was not nearly as quick as Hare. In fact, he spent a lot of his time sleeping. But Owl was a very wise and good neighbor. Sometimes he thought to himself, "Hare always seems to be rushing somewhere in a hurry. I wonder if he ever slows down?"

"How are you doing today, Owl?" yelled Hare as he ran by Owl's tree house.

"Oh, hello, Hare. I'm napping as usual," replied Owl. "Where are you off to in such a hurry?"

"I'm very busy. I have to run around the lake," said Hare. "Then I must hop over some logs. Then I'm due for some short sprints through the forest."

"Good for you, Hare," said Owl, closing his eyes again. "Have a good time."

Every afternoon, when the weather was nice, Tortoise would gather up his paints and brushes, and go out into the woods. Tortoise loved to paint pictures of the flowers, the trees, and the stream near his house. He worked slowly, but his pictures were very beautiful.

"Every stroke of my brush must be done very carefully," said Tortoise to himself.

Tortoise took a lot of time choosing which paints he would use to paint a picture. Sometimes half a day would go by before he decided which shade of green to use on the leaf of a violet flower. Then another day would go by as Tortoise mixed the perfect color to paint the petals of the violet.

"Purple is the hardest color to make," said Tortoise. "Sometimes there is just too much blue or too much red."

Hare thought painting a picture was not at all exciting. "What a dull fellow Tortoise is!" he said. "Purple is purple!"

Hare had the most fun leaping about the forest. He liked to visit his friends, rushing from house to house. Wherever he went, he always ran very, very fast.

Although Hare had many friends, there was just one problem. Hare was sure that he was the smartest, fastest, most handsome animal in the whole forest. And he never failed to tell his friends how splendid he was. "I think I look especially fine today," he would say to himself as he stood in front of the mirror.

Hare's friend Owl would just sit by and not say anything when Hare acted this way. Owl knew it was best to leave the matter alone. Hare would never sit still long enough to hear what Owl had to say anyway.

"Sometimes I think it is a shame that I have such good looks AND that I am the fastest animal in the forest," said Hare. "All the other animals must feel so jealous."

Owl just closed his eyes and pretended to be napping again.

Tortoise never bragged about himself. He knew that he was not particularly handsome and that he was very slow, but he did not mind. He was happy to spend his time working hard, painting his beautiful pictures at his very slow pace.

"I think it is better to take your time and do things right, then to rush to do ten things without doing your best," said Tortoise.

One day, Tortoise was sitting beside the road painting a picture of the pretty wildflowers he saw in the forest. Hare came up and said, "You are such a slowpoke, Tortoise. You've been working on the same picture all week!"

"I'm not slow," protested Tortoise.

"Silly fellow," said Hare. "You're so slow that I could beat you at anything you can name. Just name something, and I'll win."

"All right," said Tortoise. "How about a race?"

What an idea! Hare laughed and laughed at the thought of running a race with Tortoise. Hare laughed so hard he thought that he would explode!

"Great!" laughed Hare. "I'd gladly race you, Tortoise!"

"Fine," said Tortoise. "Then a race it is." He turned slowly back to his painting as he said this. A tiny smile crossed his face. He immediately went back to concentrating on painting the pretty wildflowers just right. He would worry about the race when the proper time came.

Hare was a little surprised that Tortoise did not seem afraid. He walked off toward home before he burst into his usual run.

Word of the race spread quickly through the forest. All the animals were talking about how Tortoise had boldly challenged Hare. "What was Tortoise thinking? Why did he do such a thing?" they wondered. "Did Tortoise really think that he could run faster than Hare?" Even Squirrel had to laugh at the idea of Tortoise racing Hare.

Squirrel hurried down her tree and went over to tell Owl the exciting news.

When Owl heard about the big race, he blinked his eyes slowly and said in his deep, wise voice, "I am not so sure that Hare will win. You never can tell what is going to happen."

Squirrel was puzzled by what Owl said. "Do you think Tortoise will win the race?" asked Squirrel.

"All I am saying is that you never can tell what will happen," said Owl again slowly.

Squirrel just scratched her head, then scurried down the tree to talk with the other animals about the race. This was the most exciting thing that had happened in the forest. Everyone would surely be watching the race!

On the day of the big race, all the animals gathered at the starting line. Skunk and Chipmunk had been busy laying out the course for the race. Bear had made a banner to mark the finish line. Squirrel had a bunch of balloons she was giving to all the animals in the crowd.

Fox was to be the judge. "If the race is close, I will say who is the winner," he declared.

"Don't worry," said Hare. "You won't have a problem. I will be so far ahead, there will be no doubt about who is the winner of the race!"

Hare did a few quick sprints to show off for the crowd. Then Hare did some fancy stretches. Tortoise jogged slowly in place.

"I don't want to pull a muscle," said Tortoise.

Hare just laughed and jumped around the crowd. He couldn't wait to get started. This was his moment to show all the animals in the forest that he was indeed the fastest animal, not that there was any doubt.

"The only muscle you might pull, Tortoise, is your neck muscle," bragged Hare, "when you see how fast I run past you!"

Tortoise and Hare stepped up to the starting line. Tortoise looked nervous when he saw all the animals watching. Hare smiled and waved to the crowd. He even winked at a few lady friends. He could hardly wait to show Tortoise a thing or two about running a race.

Fox looked at both runners. He stood in front of them and shouted, "Get ready. Get set. GO!"

The race was on! Hare dashed across the starting line. In the blink of an eye, he disappeared over the first hill.

"Oh, dear," said Squirrel to herself. "There goes Hare, out of sight already. Poor Tortoise hasn't even started!"

Sure enough, Tortoise was just beginning to climb the steep path—very slowly.

"Slow and steady. Slow and steady," said Tortoise over and over to himself. This helped to keep his mind on the race.

Hare was no longer in sight. Tortoise tried not to think about where Hare was. He just wanted to finish the race. He could do it, he thought.

"Slow and steady," Tortoise said.

Hare ran and ran until he was sure he would win. "This isn't even a race," he said to himself. "I think I'll lie down and rest a bit. Then I'll finish and still have plenty of time to spare. There's no way that slowpoke will ever catch up with me!"

So Hare lay down under a shady tree and soon fell fast asleep.

While Hare was fast asleep, Tortoise caught up. Then Tortoise passed Hare! Hare didn't even move a hair.

Suddenly Hare awoke with a start. "What was that?" he cried. He could hear cheering. He leaped to his feet and began running as fast as his long legs would carry him. But when he saw the finish line of the race, he could not believe his eyes.

Tortoise was almost at the finish line! He was about to win the race. Hare could not believe it. As he ran faster and faster, he could see Tortoise was crossing the finish line!

The crowd cheered and cheered. They ran to the finish line to congratulate Tortoise. Owl blinked his eyes and said what all the other animals were thinking, "Slow and steady wins the race!" And indeed it did!

Bookworm Library

Written by Lisa Harkrader
Illustrated by Elena Kucharik

Cora Caterpillar rushed through town. When she
reached the Bookworm Library, she unlocked the
door and hurried inside.

Cora was the head librarian. She had a long list of things to do
before the library opened.

Cora read her list. "Number one: straighten shelves."

Cora bustled up and down the rows and rows of bookshelves.
She straightened books that were leaning over. Cora picked up
fallen books from the floor. She found books that were upside
down and put them back how they belonged.

When she finished, Cora looked at the neat rows of books. "They look like an army of ants," she said proudly, "standing at attention."

Cora read her list again. "Number two: turn on computers."

Cora went to the table of computers. One by one, she pushed the buttons to turn on each computer. One by one, the trusty computers hummed to life.

Cora listened. "They're buzzing like a beehive," she said.

Cora looked at her list again. "Number three: choose two books for story hour." Cora frowned. "This will be hard. I like so many," she said to herself.

It was true. The Bookworm Library had hundreds of great books. How could she choose just two?

Cora thought about the books she loved best. She liked animal stories and funny stories and westerns and poems. Cora snapped her fingers. "I'll read a book of poems about animals and a funny book about a cowboy," she said.

Cora found the books, then looked at the clock. It was time for the library to open.

Cora unlocked the door. Young bugs from all over town raced inside. Sally Spider came with Francine Firefly. Busby Bumblebee brought Wally Waterbug and a little bitty bug, Rollie Roly-Poly.

The little bugs pulled books from the shelves. They piled lots of books on the tables. They laughed and talked and read out loud.

"Oh, my," Cora thought to herself. "How can such little bugs make such a big racket?"

Cora put her finger to her lips. "Shh," she said. Nobody heard her. "Quiet," whispered Cora. "We can't be noisy in the library." Nobody paid attention.

Cora sighed. She looked at the two books in her arms and smiled. "Does anybody want to hear a story?" Cora called out in a louder voice.

The little bugs looked at each other. "Yes!" they cheered.

The young bugs scrambled over to the story circle. They spread out on the soft carpet and plump pillows.

Cora settled into her cushy chair and began to read. The little bugs listened to the poems and the funny western story.

"I liked the butterfly and lion poem," said Busby Bumblebee.

"I liked the cowboy," said Wally Waterbug.

"I liked the cowboy's horse," said Sally Spider.

Rollie Roly-Poly didn't say anything. He was fast asleep.

Francine Firefly giggled. "Rollie must have thought we were reading bedtime stories," she said.

"Now it's time to find books to take home," said Cora.

"I want a book about weaving," said Sally Spider.

"I want a book about boats," said Wally Waterbug.

Sally and Wally and Francine and Busby went off to find books. Cora gently shook Rollie Roly-Poly.

"Time to wake up," Cora said. Rollie rubbed his eyes. "Do you want to take a book home?" Cora asked. Rollie nodded sleepily and yawned.

The little bugs all found books. They marched up to Cora's desk to check them out.

Cora wrote each little bug's name on a card in the book. She took out a big rubber stamp and stamped each card.

"You can take these books home to read," Cora said. "You can keep them for two whole weeks."

The little bugs gathered their books. They put them in their bags and filed toward the door.

"Good-bye, Sally," said Cora. "Good-bye, Wally and Busby and Francine." Cora stopped. Where was Rollie?

"Has anyone seen Rollie?" Cora asked the children. Sally and Wally and Busby and Francine shook their heads.

"Help me find him," said Cora.

Cora looked under the tables. Sally looked by the humming computers. Francine and Wally and Busby looked behind the bookshelves. No Rollie.

"Where did he go?" Cora asked.

"The last time I saw him," said Francine, "he was sleeping on a pillow in the story circle."

Cora smiled and hurried to the story circle. There was Rollie, curled up in Cora's big chair, fast asleep.

Cora chuckled at the snug little bug. "I guess my bedtime stories really work," she said.

Cora woke Rollie and helped him check out a book. Then she sent the children home.

"I love being a librarian," Cora said.

Princess and the Pea

Adapted by Eric Fein
Illustrated by Anthony Lewis

L ong ago and far away there lived a lonely prince. He
spent endless days traveling from one kingdom to
another kingdom in hopes of finding a real princess to
be his wife.

But every noble lady he met turned out to be unacceptable. It
was not that the women were not beautiful or smart, for they
were. It was that none of the women had those certain special
qualities that made them real princesses. The prince would only
marry a real princess.

After each journey the prince would return home to the castle.

The king and queen worried about their son and did their best to raise his spirits.

"I know!" said the king. "We will invite all the wonderful women from every kingdom to the palace for a festival."

The royal family held the festival as promised, and hundreds of young women came with the hopes of marrying the prince. But it was no use. The prince found something wrong with every one of them. They all returned home disappointed.

One night, a terrible storm fell over the kingdom. Thunder bellowed, and lightning lit up the sky. Among the few souls unfortunate enough to be caught in the storm was a fair maiden on her way home. The young lady's carriage had lost a wheel.

"We shall seek shelter in that castle," the princess told her driver. "I'm sure they will help us."

At the castle, the prince had been preparing for bed when he heard a knock at the door. Not being very sleepy, he thought he would answer the door himself.

"Forgive our intrusion, Your Highness," said the princess as she stood in the doorway, dripping wet.

The prince was stunned at the sight of this maiden.

"I am a princess. My carriage has lost its wheel. We have no place to stay," she said. "Will you help us?"

Despite her muddy, rain-soaked appearance, the prince liked this young woman and wanted to help.

"Of course you may stay here," the prince said. "Come, allow me to show you to the fireplace, where you may warm yourself before you catch a cold."

"Thank you. That is very kind of you," said the princess.

Then the queen said, "While you warm yourself by the fire, I shall oversee the preparations for your stay in our guest room."

"You are all so good to me," said the princess. "Thank you."

The queen just smiled. She was skeptical as to whether the young lady was truly a princess. To find out, she devised a test.

The servants piled twenty mattresses, one on top of the other. Then they put twenty fine quilts, one over the other, on top of the twenty mattresses. So soft and lush was the bed that any ordinary person would sleep forever. Then the queen placed a small uncooked pea under the bottom mattress.

"If she is truly a princess, she'll get no comfort out of this bed. For only the delicate nature of a true princess will be able to feel the hardness of the pea under all these layers," said the queen.

The prince and the princess talked for quite a while before turning in for the night. They enjoyed each other's company very much and went to bed smiling.

When the princess arrived at the guest room, she saw the exquisite bed arranged for her to sleep in. The princess climbed into the tall bed and lay down. As soon as she did, she felt that something was not right. She turned onto her right side and then onto her left. It did not help. She tried lying on her stomach, but that did not help either. She tried to sleep with her head on the opposite side of the bed, and diagonally, too. Nothing worked.

"Oh, dear," said the princess. "How will I sleep in such an uncomfortable bed?"

The princess continued to toss and turn all night. She felt as though there were a boulder underneath her blanket. She could not understand why the royal family would have such lumpy bedding in their guest room.

The next morning, the princess joined the royal family for breakfast. The queen asked her how she had slept.

"The bed was truly lovely and soft," she said. "But I could feel something hard underneath it. It had me tossing all night."

The queen began to get excited at what she was hearing.

"Finally," continued the princess, "I got out of bed and started looking under each mattress, one at a time. You will not believe what I found underneath the bottom mattress—a pea!" said the princess, holding up the pea.

The queen leaned over to the prince and whispered, "She is indeed a true princess. Only a true maiden, noble born and bred, would feel such discomfort from a tiny pea."

The prince was very happy with this news, for he had fallen in love with the princess. He got down on one knee and proposed marriage.

The princess accepted, for she had fallen in love with the prince, too. The prince and princess had a very large wedding at the castle. There were feasts and fireworks in celebration. The prince and the true princess lived happily ever after.

Camp Out

Written by Sarah Toast
Illustrated by Joe Veno

David and Liz have work to do. After a long hike, they have arrived at the edge of the woods with all their camping gear packed in backpacks.

Now they have to pitch camp. First they stretch a rope between two trees and tie it tight. Then they make a tent with the blanket they brought along. Liz is very careful to hold the ends tight while David pulls the blanket over the rope.

"Great work!" David says to Liz. The tent looks perfect. David and Liz think setting up camp is fun, especially when they work together.

After hiking and setting up camp, David and Liz are hungry. Even though it is fun, it is still hard work. They settle down in the tent and open their backpacks. They take out sandwiches and apples to eat for lunch. They drink grape juice from canteens.

"These sandwiches are yummy!" says Liz.

"Everything tastes better when you are camping," says David. "I think it's the fresh air."

David takes his binoculars out of his pack. He looks outside the tent for wild animals.

"All clear!" says David. "No wild animals."

"Wait! Here's one!" Liz takes her teddy bear out of her pink backpack. She tells her brave teddy bear to guard the campsite while they go off to look for adventure. "Our stuff will be safe with Teddy on guard," she tells David.

"I can't wait to go exploring," says David.

"I'm ready. Pack up any extra sandwiches and grape juice just in case we get lost in the desert," says Liz.

"Good idea," says David.

Then David and Liz are on their way to explore the wild.

David and Liz walk quietly so they can listen carefully for any wild animals.

"What's that?" asks David. He hears something in the bushes behind him. Liz hears it, too.

"Let's just keep walking," says Liz. When they look back, they see a tiny kitten sneaking out of the bushes.

"Oh, no. A tiger!" says David. "He sure looks ferocious!"

They both giggle and continue their hike.

"Meow!" says the tiger.

"I wonder what other wild animals we'll see on our adventure," says Liz. "I hope we don't run into any more tigers."

"Maybe we should have brought Teddy with us to protect us from danger," laughs David.

"I think even Teddy would be scared of a tiger," says Liz.

As they walk, David and Liz think of Teddy. They are glad that he is back at camp. He wouldn't like hiking too much. He is a stay-put teddy bear. Besides, he doesn't have any hiking boots!

Soon David and Liz forget about the tiger and Teddy, too. There are so many things to look at as they walk.

Liz and David walk for a long time. Just when they begin to get tired, they find sturdy branches that are just the right size for walking sticks.

"These are perfect," says David.

"I'm not so tired anymore!" says Liz.

They walk up to a big log lying across their path. Then Liz sees something moving on the other side of the log.

Liz and David walk up to the log very quietly. On the other side is a white rabbit nibbling delicious grass. The rabbit looks at the two explorers, then it scampers away.

"Did you see how close we came to that wild animal?" says Liz. "I'm glad it didn't bite us!" Liz and David laugh.

"Yeah. But I think that bunny was more scared of us than we were of him," says David.

David and Liz use their walking sticks to help them get over the log. When David stands on top of the log, he says, "Hey! I can see for miles up here!"

"Can you see Alaska?" asks Liz.

"I think so!" says David.

When David climbs over the log, the two are on their way to continue their adventure.

"We've seen a tiger and a rabbit," says David. "Let's look closely at the ground and find more wild animals."

David and Liz walk and look, but they do not see any more animals. Liz thinks she sees a bug, but it is just a rock. Finally, they find two beautiful blue feathers on the ground. Liz looks up to see where the feathers fell from.

"I see a bird's nest!" she exclaims. "The mother bird is taking care of three baby birds."

"Let's get a closer look," says David. He gets the binoculars out of his pack so they can see the birds better.

The babies are very young. They call out to their mother. "Peep, peep, chirp, chirp," say the baby birds.

"Chirp, chirp, to you, baby birds!" says Liz. "They are very cute. I think they must be hungry."

"Mama bird will go get worms for the babies to eat," says David. "Baby birds like to eat worms."

"Yuck," says Liz. "I'd rather have a sandwich."

The explorers keep hiking until they come to a great lake—well, a pond, at least. Liz and David agree that crossing the pond will be tough.

First, they take off their backpacks and slide the straps onto their walking sticks. Then they take off their shoes and socks and roll up their pants. They balance all their gear on their heads and fearlessly slosh from one shore of the lake—well, pond—to the other. The water feels cool on their feet, and the mud feels good between their toes.

"Good thing Teddy isn't here," says Liz. "He hates mud."

David and Liz laugh as they splash the water with their feet. They see who can make the biggest splash.

"Be careful," says David. "Don't get our hiking gear wet."

When the two are safely on the other side of the pond, they put their socks and shoes back on. They roll down their pants and put on their backpacks. Then they are ready to keep on walking.

"That water felt good on my tired feet," says Liz.

"Now I am ready to hike forever," says David.

The two friends laugh and talk as they walk. No sooner do they start exploring again then they see something exciting.

"Muddy tracks!" says Liz.

"They look like bear tracks to me," says David.

The two trackers look at each other and think a minute before they decide. "Let's follow those tracks!" they both say.

"I wonder where those tracks will lead," says Liz.

"I think I saw a bear's den by the lake we crossed," says David. "Maybe the bear is going exploring, too."

"From the looks of his tracks, he's not wearing any hiking boots," says Liz.

"Maybe it is Teddy!" says David. Liz and David laugh as they think of Teddy out on his own expedition.

David and Liz look closely at the tracks as they continue to follow the trail. As they walk, they have a feeling that they are getting close to the wild animal that left the muddy footprints. The two friends begin to feel a little nervous.

"I hope it is Teddy," says Liz.

"I hope it is as friendly as Teddy, anyway," says David.

David and Liz follow the tracks through the grass. It gets harder and harder not to lose the trail. They stop in their own tracks when they see that the bear tracks lead right to their tent!

David laughs and runs to the tent. "Come on, Liz! This animal won't hurt us!" he says.

Just then they hear David's mom calling to them.

"Hi, little campers," says David's mom. "I thought I'd let Bingo out to play with you in the yard. He's waiting for you inside the tent. He wants to camp, too."

Bingo is David's new puppy.

Liz, David, and Bingo play in the warm, safe tent for the rest of the day.

"Let's build a rocket and fly to the moon tomorrow," says Liz. "Bingo can come, too!"

"I'll bring my binoculars," says David.

Little Red Hen

Adapted by Jennifer Boudart
Illustrated by Linda Dockey Graves

The little red hen lived next to the road by the farmer's house. Where she lived wasn't very fancy, but she loved it. She shared her home with her five baby chicks and her friends, the dog, the cat, and the duck.

The little red hen worked very hard. She kept the house and the yard neat and clean.

Everyone liked having a clean house and good food on the table. When it came time to do the chores, though, the other animals always seemed to disappear. The little red hen did all the work herself.

One day, the little red hen was sweeping her yard. When she looked down on the ground, she found some kernels of wheat. She put the kernels into a basket for safe keeping. Then she went to look for the dog, the cat, and the duck.

She found the dog, the cat, and the duck by the pond. She showed them the kernels that she had found and asked, "Who will help me plant these?"

Her three friends looked at each other. Then they looked at the little red hen.

"Not I," said the dog.

"Not I," said the cat.

"Not I," said the duck.

"Then I'll plant them myself," she told them. The little red hen returned to the garden and began digging.

Soon her baby chicks came to see what she was doing. They told her they wanted to help. The little red hen and her five baby chicks pretended they were burying treasure. The game made the work go quickly. The little chicks had fun scratching and digging in the dirt. Soon they had planted all the kernels.

The little red hen visited the garden every day to watch the wheat grow. She made sure the young plants got plenty of bright sunlight and care.

One day, she saw many weeds growing in the garden. She found her three friends leaning against the farmer's barn. The little red hen said, "There are weeds that are stopping the wheat from growing. Will you help me pull the weeds?"

"I can't," said the cat. "They're all dirty. Do you have any idea how long it takes me to wash my paws?"

The dog said, "I need to take a nap."

And the duck just quacked and waddled off to the pond.

No one would help. "I'll just do it myself," said the little red hen. Then she walked back to the garden. Once again, her chicks joined her. They said that they wanted to help her to pull the weeds. They had a contest to see who could pull the most weeds. It was such fun that they finished in no time. Some of the weeds were quite tasty, too!

At the end of the day, the little red hen and her chicks were tired, but they felt good knowing that the wheat would grow.

A dry spell kept the rain away for a week. The little red hen was worried about the wheat. If the plants did not get some water soon, the tender stalks would wither and die. The only thing to do was bring water to the plants. She went looking for her friends. She found them on top of the hay pile. The hen looked up and said, "The summer heat is too strong for the wheat. Who will help me water the garden?"

The dog, the cat, and the duck looked down at her. "We're busy writing a song and can't be bothered now," growled the dog. "Didn't you hear me playing my banjo?"

"I'll just water it myself," she said. The little red hen took her watering pail to the garden. Her five chicks came to keep her company. The hen pretended to be a thundercloud and tried to sprinkle them with water. Before long, the whole garden had been watered.

The summer sun was very good, and the wheat grew fast. The little red hen and her chicks visited the garden every day. They lovingly tended to the wheat, and it grew strong and hardy. There was going to be a bumper crop!

Soon it was fall and the wheat turned golden brown. The little red hen knew what that meant. She found her friends playing cards under the farmer's wagon. The hen knelt down and said, "Who will help me harvest the wheat?"

The dog, the cat, and the duck kept their eyes on their cards.

"Not I!" said the dog. "I have a full house."

"Not I!" said the cat. "I'm the dealer."

"Not I!" said the duck. "Wheat makes me sneeze."

The hen stood up and fixed her apron. "Then I'll harvest it myself," she said. The little red hen took her cutting tools to the garden. This time the five chicks were waiting for her. The family cut the wheat and tied it into bundles. They pretended that the wheat stalks were long strands of spaghetti. They were going to make the biggest dish of spaghetti and meatballs ever. They sang songs, and soon the hard work was done.

Even though she had already spent a great deal of time and energy on the garden, the little red hen knew the work was not finished. She often told her chicks that if a job was worth doing, it was worth doing well.

The wheat was now ready to be taken to the mill. The little red hen went looking for her friends. She found them sitting by the road. "I need to have the wheat ground into flour," she said. "Who will help me carry it to the miller?"

The dog, the cat, and the duck looked way down the road. The miller was located several miles away.

"Not I!" said the dog. "It's too far."

"Not I!" said the cat. "My feet hurt just thinking about it."

"Not I!" said the duck. "I stubbed my toe earlier."

"I see!" said the little red hen.

Once again, the little red hen would have to do it herself. She and her chicks left right away. They had a long journey ahead of them, and the chicks moved slowly. The trip seemed to go much faster when they pretended to be traveling with their knapsacks across the country.

The friendly miller greeted them on the road. "That's quite a crop of wheat you have. It was a good year," he said.

"Yes, and it was a lot of work to harvest," said the little red hen. "But the fresh bread will be worth it."

The little red hen returned home. She and the chicks were so tired that they soon fell asleep. That night everyone slept very well. The next morning, the little red hen went outside. Her friends were sunbathing on the roof. She called to them, "Who will help me bake bread with my flour?"

The dog, the cat, and the duck didn't even bother looking down at the little red hen.

"Not I!" said the dog. "It's a beautiful day. Who would want to be indoors baking bread?"

"Not I!" said the cat. "I have sunbathing to do."

"Not I!" said the duck. "All that flour will get my feathers dusty, and I just went swimming!"

The hen shook her head. She thought, Who would want to spend all day doing nothing? She told the three, "I'll bake it myself." The little red hen went inside. Her chicks tried to make the bread dough for her. Flour was all over the floor and the chicks, too. They shaped the dough into a big loaf and pretended to be sculptors making a statue. Everyone was sorry to have to stop when the loaf was finished.

Soon the smell of baking bread floated in the air. The dog, the cat, and the duck came and looked into the kitchen. Two baby chicks danced around the little red hen.

"Who will help me eat this tasty, fresh bread?" asked the little red hen.

"I will!" said the dog.

"I will!" said the cat.

"I will!" said the duck.

"Well," said the little red hen, "anyone who helped make this bread can have some. So, if you helped plant the wheat, water it, weed it, harvest it, take it to the miller, or bake the bread, raise your hand!"

All five chicks raised their little wings. That night, six tummies got their fill of bread as a reward for work well done.

The dog, the cat, and the duck were left in the yard feasting only on the wonderful smells.

The Pied Piper of Hamelin

Adapted by Carolyn Quattrocki
Illustrated by Tim Ellis

O nce upon a time, far away and long ago, there was a town called Hamelin. It was a pleasant little town with a river on one side and a mountain on the other.

The people of Hamelin liked living there. They always had plenty to eat and drink. Their children were healthy and happy.

One day, the people of Hamelin saw that they had a very serious problem. Their lovely town was full of rats! Everywhere the people went, there were rats. Rats were in the trees, the streets, the alleys, the attics, and the cellars. There were even rats on the tops of houses.

Rats went into the kitchens and bothered the cooks. The rats nibbled the bread and cakes. They ate the cheeses, drank the soup, and ruined the pies.

As soon as one rat was chased away, three more came to take its place! The rats appeared almost as if by magic.

Rats fought with dogs and bit the cats. Even the mice were scared of the rats! Those rats made their nests everywhere in town, even in the gentlemen's hats. They were so noisy that ladies having their tea together could scarcely hear each other's voices.

What on earth were the poor people of Hamelin to do?

There were rats in shoes. There were rats in socks. Nothing stopped the rats, not even big locks! Rats got into the wallpaper and under the cupboards. Soon it seemed that there were more rats in Hamelin than people!

"What are we going to do?" people shouted.

"Rats! Rats! There are too many rats!" screamed John Benny.

"I can't sleep," said Joyce Teapot. "The rats make too much noise! Even my cat can't sleep!"

It seemed that the people of Hamelin were losing hope.

The most important man in the town was the mayor. It was his job to see that everything ran smoothly. The mayor was a wealthy man who loved to eat the richest food and drink the finest wine. When he went out on the town, he wore a cape of fur, a cap of fine feathers, and costly rings on his fingers. He thought himself a splendid fellow. Even his everyday clothes were made of the finest cloths from around the world. He never went anywhere without his jewels. He even wore them in the bathtub!

To help the mayor with his job of running the town, there was a town council. The mayor and his council met each week to talk about all the things that needed to be done in the town. The weekly meetings in the town hall were usually festive occasions. They always had a feast of good food and wine.

And where there was food and wine, the rats had come to feast, too. The rat problem in the town of Hamelin had even invaded the town council meeting. But because the mayor was so wealthy, he always had plenty of food for himself, the council members, and two dozen rats.

The rats were not a problem for the mayor. Not yet.

One day, the townspeople said to themselves, "We have had enough of these rats in our town! The mayor and his council sit and do nothing, while the rats are everywhere. Something must be done!"

With that, a large crowd of people gathered before the town hall and cried out, "Let us see the mayor!"

In his office the mayor sat behind his large golden desk and listened to the people's complaints. He knew how awful it was to have rats everywhere in town. His own house had become full of them as well.

Sadly, the mayor did not have the slightest idea of how to fix the problem. None of the members of his council did either. They had never dealt with a problem this big before.

The townspeople did not care. They wanted this problem solved. They grew angrier and angrier.

The mayor felt helpless. He did not like it when people were angry with him. He thought he might have to have the royal jeweler make him a shiny new ring to cheer him up.

"But what about the town?" cried the townspeople.

Suddenly, there was a knock on the mayor's door. The people all turned to see a strange fellow standing there. He was wearing a long, red cape and a hat with a red feather. He had yellow hair, and a pipe hung from a silk scarf around his neck.

"I am just a poor piper," he said, "but I can rid your town of rats. Would you pay a hundred pieces of gold for me to do it?"

"Oh, I would give a thousand pieces of gold to anyone who could rid us of these rats!" exclaimed the mayor.

The rest of the council members echoed, "Yes, yes. A thousand pieces of gold!"

All the townspeople heard this and began to get excited!

"A thousand pieces of gold!" shouted John Benny.

"Finally, someone is here to help!" shouted Tom Castle.

"Now I can get some sleep!" cried Joyce Teapot.

The piper began to dance around the room. Everyone cheered as he danced.

"I will be happy to help you with the rats!" he told them all.

The crowd cheered even louder when the piper danced toward the door. He was the town hero!

The pied piper stepped into the town square and began to play a tune on his pipe. How beautiful and sweet was his music!

Suddenly rats came running to him from all directions. Big rats, small rats, thin rats, fat rats, old rats, and young rats came running. Rats came out from behind the wallpaper. They came out from under the cupboards. They ignored the ladies having tea and joined the other rats. Before long, the pied piper had a whole army of rats behind him.

Through the town and to the edge of the river, all the rats followed the pied piper. At the river's edge he paused, but the rats kept running. Without stopping, every single rat jumped into the river. The swift river current quickly swept all the rats away from the town of Hamelin.

The people were astonished. All the rats were gone! They cheered as the piper walked back to the town hall. Several people gathered up the pied piper and put him up on their shoulders.

He was the town's hero indeed!

Now it seemed that the people of Hamelin did not have to worry about rats anymore. They were free.

The pied piper was then set down before the king. To the astonished mayor the pied piper said, "I have come to collect my thousand pieces of gold."

"But sir," cried the mayor, "that was only a joke! Surely you could not expect us to pay a thousand pieces of gold for such short work. Here are twenty-five pieces."

"You promised one thousand," said the pied piper.

"All right, here are fifty pieces. Take them and be gone," said the mayor.

The piper was very angry. None of the town council members said a thing. The people of Hamelin were quiet. They did not know what to do. They could see the piper growing angry. But whatever the mayor said, they would not challenge.

Suddenly, the pied piper began to play his pipe again. All the people of the town were confused. Were the rats going to come back from the river? They did not know what was happening. The piper went down to the town square as he played his pipe.

This time the children heard the music and came running to him from all directions.

Before the pied piper had finished a whole song on his pipe, the sound of many small running feet could be heard.

The children listened, and the beautiful music was so sweet to their ears that they could not help themselves. They ran to the place where the pied piper was playing.

From each street more children came. Small children, large children, brothers, sisters, and little babies carried by the older children, they all ran to the pied piper. Little hands clapped to the music. Small feet danced to the merry tune. What a parade they made! A long line of dancing children had formed behind the pied piper.

Soon all the children in the town were following the pied piper. He led them toward the river. The people were suddenly more afraid than confused. Would their children jump in the river as the rats had done?

The people began to beg the mayor to do something. The piper was leading their children out of town. Something needed to be done to save their children.

The mayor only stood in amazement. He was helpless.

The pied piper turned and headed toward the mountain. The people thought he would never be able to lead their children over such a high mountain.

Just then, the pied piper and the long line of dancing children reached the mountain. The townspeople were quite amazed as a magical door suddenly opened in the side of the rock.

As the townspeople watched, the pied piper led all the children of Hamelin through the door in the mountain.

The poor people of Hamelin cried as they watched the pied piper lead their children through the door, never to be seen again. They were sad for what their mayor had done. Because he was selfish and greedy, the children of the town were gone. The mayor had plenty of money to give the piper. But now it was too late. There were no more children in Hamelin.

The children of Hamelin went to live beyond the mountain in a land that was always filled with happiness and laughter and sunshine, and definitely no rats!

Patch's Lucky Star

Written by Brian Conway
Illustrated by Loretta Lustig

Patch was a pretty little turtle who lived by the pond. She was as quiet and careful as a turtle could be. Most turtles her age romped along the shores of the pond all day, but Patch did not.

Patch looked just like any other young turtle she knew, except for one thing. She had a yellow patch on the outside of her shell. Patch was the only turtle at the pond to have such a shell. "It is such an odd shell for a turtle to have," Patch thought to herself.

"It's not odd," Patch's mother would tell her often. "It's just different. It makes you special, Patch."

Patch did not want to be special. She just wanted a normal shell so everyone would stop looking at her patch.

Patch would hide away most of the day among the tall grasses around the pond. Sometimes she would creep and crawl to her favorite spots on the pond, but only when she was sure there was nobody around.

Most days, Patch just tucked herself up inside her shell and stayed there. Patch liked staying inside her shell very much. Inside it was dark and quiet. Inside Patch could be all alone.

Patch didn't have to worry about getting splashed by frogs or being sniffed by the bigger animals that came to drink from the pond. And if any of the other animals were looking at her odd shell, Patch didn't want to see their stares.

Most of all, though, she didn't want to have to look at her own shell. She thought the big yellow patch was terrible. In fact, she thought it made her whole shell look terrible. So Patch stayed inside her shell where she did not have to see it or anything else.

Patch stayed there and daydreamed. In her dreams, she would stick her head out proudly and walk in the flower patch.

Patch dreamed that she would go from flower to flower like a bee and smell the wonderful smells.

From the darkness of her shell, Patch also imagined that she had great adventures. She saw herself zipping and diving from shore to shore like a dragonfly.

One day, Diamond and Snapper walked by Patch's hiding place. She hoped the two young turtles would not notice her, but they came up and tapped on her shell.

"Patch!" they called. "Come exploring with us."

Patch stayed very still in her shell. Soon they went away.

Patch pretended she went exploring with them. She thought about finding a cool, shady place where she could slide down a great big log and splash into the pond.

Later that day, Patch heard her mother's voice outside her shell. Poking her head out, Patch was surprised to see Diamond and Snapper's mother there, too.

"Have you seen Diamond or Snapper?" Patch's mother asked. "They've been gone for hours."

"They went exploring," Patch told her.

Diamond and Snapper's mother shook her head. "We'll have to go looking for those two," she said. "It's getting dark."

"You stay here, Patch," her mother said. "We do not need another lost turtle."

Patch shivered, glad she had stayed inside her shell. She thought it must be scary to be lost on the pond at night. Then she saw that the stars were starting to glitter in the dark sky.

"If only my shell could shine as brightly as the stars," she thought aloud. "Then I wouldn't mind my patch so much."

As Patch sighed, she heard Diamond and Snapper calling for their mother. Their mother called back to them. Their voices were coming closer to Patch's place on the shore.

Patch quickly ducked back into her shell. Soon it seemed that all the turtles were just outside, huddled around her. Everyone was talking all at once.

"We kept going in circles," Snapper said.

"Everything looked the same in the dark," added Diamond. "But then we saw Patch's bright yellow patch all the way across the pond."

"We followed Patch's patch all the way back!" said Snapper.

"Thank goodness for that patch!" their mother said.

"If you ever get lost again," Diamond and Snapper's mother said, "be sure you follow the North Star."

She pointed up to the brightest star in the sky.

"We don't need the North Star," Snapper said. "We've got our own star right here on the shore!"

"And it's the brightest star on the pond. That's for sure!" said Diamond.

"Patch," her mother said, "they're talking about your special shell."

Patch was so happy, her shell couldn't hold her. She popped out and looked back at her patch. In the moonlight, it did shine brightly!

Tomorrow Patch would come out again to see just how much it really did shine. She hoped her star would shine all the time. It was a very special patch indeed.

Little Quack

Written by Catherine McCafferty
Illustrated by Kurt Mitchell

It was Little Quack's first day on the pond! There were
so many new things to see and explore.

"Little Quack, go to the back!" his sisters said.
"You're holding up the line."

"Okay," said Little Quack.

Little Quack didn't mind going to the back of the line. It gave
him more time to look at things.

Little Quack was always curious. When his family swam on the
water, Little Quack dipped under it. When a creature under the
water blew bubbles, Little Quack blew some back.

His family kept paddling along. Little Quack did not notice that they were swimming away. They did not seem to notice that Little Quack stayed behind to play.

When Little Quack popped above water again, his family was nowhere in sight. Little Quack looked around. All the new things at the pond seemed a little scary now. Little Quack would feel better if his family were there. How would he find them?

Little Quack paddled in a slow circle. A strange green animal with a loud, deep voice watched him. As a fly buzzed past, the strange green animal's tongue shot out. *Z-z-zip-p-p!* He caught the fly. Little Quack backed up. What if the green animal caught him?

The green animal laughed as Little Quack back-paddled. "Don't worry, Ducky," the animal said. "I'm a frog. I eat bugs, not ducks."

That made Little Quack feel better. "Hello, Frog," he said. "I'm looking for my family. Have you seen them?"

"I only look for flies, not ducks," croaked Frog. "You should ask Bluebird. She sees everything on the pond."

"Bluebird?" Little Quack said to himself.

He wondered if Frog was playing a joke on him. Little Quack had never heard of a bluebird before. His mother had some blue feathers, but the rest of her was a lovely brown. Little Quack wished he could see his mother's feathers right now.

"I guess I will keep looking," Little Quack said.

As he paddled along, Little Quack saw some blue feathers. He hurried toward them.

But it was not his mother. It was the bluebird! Little Quack stared at her. She looked so different, but pretty.

"Hello, little one," Bluebird chirped. Her voice was a sweet, lovely song.

"No, my name is Little Quack," the duckling told her.

Bluebird laughed. "Where is your family, Little Quack?" she asked.

"I don't know," said Little Quack. "Frog says that you can help me find them. Do you know where they are?"

"Wait here," said Bluebird. "I'll look."

Bluebird flew off, but was not gone for long. She landed on a cattail by Little Quack.

"Did you find them?" asked Little Quack.

"Your family is just over there," Bluebird said as she pointed with her wing.

Little Quack followed her direction and paddled off. But the shore all looked the same now. Little Quack could not tell if he was going in the right direction.

Little Quack looked all around, but he could not find his mother and he could not see the bluebird. And worst of all, a strange animal was watching him from the shore!

Little Quack backed away. The animal got closer to the water.

"Hi there!" the animal called. "Were you born this spring, too?"

"I was hatched, not born," he said. "Who are you?"

The animal laughed. "I'm Fox Kit."

"Why don't you have feathers?" asked Little Quack.

"Foxes don't have feathers," Fox Kit said. "We have fur."

Poor Fox Kit, Little Quack thought to himself. It must be hard not to have feathers.

"Everyone in my family has feathers," said Little Quack.
"If you want, we could all give you some. But first I have to find my family."

Fox Kit smiled. He didn't seem so strange anymore. "That's all right," he said. "I think I saw your family on the other side of these cattails."

"Thank you," said Little Quack.

Little Quack swam as fast as he could. He did not stop to explore, he did not look up at the trees, and he did not take a dip under the water. Little Quack went straight to the other side of the cattails, and there was his family!

"Mother!" Little Quack called. He was so happy to see her and his sisters.

His mother lifted her wing and Little Quack swam underneath it. He nuzzled his mother's fine feathers.

"I didn't know where you were," said Little Quack.

"I always knew where you were," his mother said. "I never lost sight of you and I never will, for you are my Little Quack."

Hello Neighbors

Written by Sarah Toast
Illustrated by Joe Veno

This is the most exciting day of Danny's life. His mom and dad just bought him a brand-new bicycle. It is shiny and red and has training wheels, which help Danny stay balanced while he learns to ride his first bike.

"Go ahead and ride around the block, Danny. We will be right behind you if you need help," says his mom. Danny pushes off and starts to pedal down the sidewalk.

At first his new bike feels wobbly, but soon he is pedaling a straight path down the sidewalk.

"Whee! Look at me!" says Danny.

Danny sees the mailman up ahead. He zooms past to show
how fast he can go on his new bike.

"Hello!" says Danny.

"Whoa!" says the mailman. "That's a fast bike you've got there!
Are you the Pony Express?"

"Yes! And I have a special delivery of fun!" calls Danny.

Next Danny sees the garbage collector. Danny is careful not to
knock over the trash cans the garbage collector is emptying.

"Hello!" says Danny.

"I'll trade you a can of trash for that bike," laughs the garbage
collector as Danny speeds by.

"No, thank you," calls Danny. "I like my bike just fine."

The garbage collector just smiles and waves as Danny rides
away. There is a lot more garbage to collect today.

Danny rides faster. He tries to weave in and out between two
sticks. His bike wobbles a little, and Danny decides to keep his
wheels straight.

"No fancy stuff just yet," says Danny to himself. "Right now I
need to worry about not falling down."

Danny pulls into the gas station on the corner. He wants to show his new bike to Bill who works there. Danny rides over the cord that makes a bell ring inside the station. Bump, bump goes his bicycle. Ding, ding goes the gas station bell.

Bill walks outside to see who his customer is.

"Hello!" says Danny.

"Hello, Danny! That's a fine bicycle you're riding. How about some air in those new tires?" asks Bill. He shows Danny how to use the air hose and sends him on his way.

"Thanks, Bill!" calls Danny. "How much do I owe you?"

"The air is free! Just be careful as you ride, Danny," says Bill.

"I will! Thank you again, Bill!" says Danny as he rides away.

Danny thinks about Bill's job at the gas station. He cannot wait until he needs to put more air in his tires. Next time, Danny will do it by himself!

Danny begins to ride fast again. He likes the feeling of the fresh air on his face as he rides. His legs feel a little tired, but he wants to keep riding. This is the most fun Danny has ever had!

"I love my bike!" calls Danny into the wind.

Danny rides past the neighborhood grocery store and slows down. "Hello!" says Danny to the grocer.

The grocer says, "Your bike is as shiny and red as my apples. Catch!" He tosses an apple to Danny. Danny stops his bike to catch the apple.

"Thank you very much," says Danny. He starts to pedal again.

"You're welcome, Danny," says the grocer. "The first apple is always free to little boys with new bikes."

Danny speeds away holding the apple. He feels so grown-up. But riding his bike with only one hand is a little tricky. Danny stops his bike and waits for his parents to catch up.

"Danny, are you having fun riding your new bike?" asks his mother when she catches up.

"Oh, I am having a great time," says Danny. "But I am having trouble carrying the apple that the grocer gave me. Will you carry it for me until we get home?"

"Why, sure," says Danny's father.

"Thank you," says Danny as he starts to pedal once again. Soon he has left his parents behind.

Danny slows down at the next corner of his block. A police officer is there directing traffic and helping people cross the street. Danny knows he is not supposed to cross the busy street, but he likes to see the police officer at work. He stops and says, "Hello!"

"Look both ways before crossing the street on that new bike," says the police officer.

"I'm not crossing the street today. I'm just going around the block to show my new bike to my neighborhood friends," says Danny with a wave.

"Thanks for stopping to say hello," says the police officer. "Now be careful."

"Thank you. I will," says Danny.

As Danny rides off on his bike, he thinks about what it would be like to be a police officer. "I would like to be one of those police officers that rides a bike," thinks Danny. "I'm sure by the time I am old enough to be a police officer, I will not need training wheels anymore."

Danny pretends he is looking for criminals as he rides his bike down the block. A squirrel gathering nuts looks suspicious.

Danny pedals past his neighbor who has a pretty flower garden in her yard. She is standing outside for the daily watering.

"Hello!" says Danny.

"That new bike is as pretty as a rose," smiles the lady as she sprays water on her flowers. She accidentally waters Danny, too. "Oh, dear. I'm sorry, Danny," she says.

"That's okay. It's just like a car wash," laughs Danny. He waves to the lady and rides off. It isn't long before he is almost completely dry as he rides through the wind.

Danny looks back to see the wet tire marks his bike makes along the sidewalk. He thinks about making wavy lines and designs, but then remembers how wobbly he still is on his bike.

"My tire tracks look like there is a giant snake following me!" says Danny to himself. "I better ride faster before the snake catches up!" Danny pretends to be scared and rides even faster.

Soon Danny is tired, though, and slows down. The snake must be long gone by now, he thinks. Danny rests his legs for a little while, then gets a sudden burst of energy.

"I'm riding faster than ever!" says Danny.

Danny rides past the firehouse just in time to see the firefighters pull up in the fire truck. "Hello!" says Danny.

"You're going so fast you could be going to a fire!" they say.

Danny laughs and imagines that his red bicycle is a big, red fire truck. He pretends that he is going to a fire!

"Woo-woo, beep, beep! Watch out everyone! I'm a fireman!" calls Danny. Danny thinks that after he puts out the fire he will rescue a cat from a tree. "After that I'll practice sliding down the pole at the firehouse," says Danny.

Danny is almost home when he rides past people working in the street. "Hello!" says Danny.

"Nice wheels, kid!" says one of the friendly workers.

"Thank you. What are you doing in the street?" asks Danny.

The workers explain that they are replacing a broken pipe that is underneath the street.

"Wow! Sounds like hard work," says Danny.

"It's not as hard as learning to ride a bike," says a worker. "Take good care of your bicycle!"

"I will!" promises Danny as he rides on.

When Danny gets closer to home he sees his best friend, Ralph. Ralph has a new bike, too. Ralph's bike is blue.

"Let's go around the block so you can show your new bike to the neighbors," says Danny. "There are lots of friendly people on our block who like bicycles."

"That would be great!" says Ralph.

"Sometimes it is fun to pretend that your bike is something else," says Danny.

"Sometimes I pretend that my bike is a horse, and I am a cowboy riding on the range," says Ralph.

"That sounds like fun! I'll ride on my horse, too, and we can pretend that we are herding cattle," says Danny.

"Good idea!" says Ralph.

And that's just what they do. The two cowboys ride off on their bikes into the sunset.

The Goose Girl

Adapted by Lisa Harkrader
Illustrated by Cindy Salans Rosenheim

Once there was a princess named Elizabeth who had promised to marry a prince she had never seen. The princess's mother, a kind and generous queen, prepared Elizabeth for her new home.

The queen chose a waiting woman named Zelda to look after the princess on her journey.

Then the queen gave Elizabeth one last gift. "This is my royal ring," said the queen. "When you arrive at your new castle, this ring will prove who you are."

"Oh, thank you so much, Mother," said Elizabeth.

Elizabeth's bags were loaded onto her faithful horse, Falada. Princess Elizabeth spoke to Falada, and the horse spoke back.

"Oh, Falada, I'm afraid. I've never done anything on my own. What if I get lost? What if I get to the kingdom, and the prince and the king don't think I'm worthy?"

"You are the most worthy person I know," said Falada. "And the prince will be charmed by your kind heart and grace."

Princess Elizabeth and Zelda set off. Elizabeth rode on Falada while Zelda rode a sure-footed old mare.

After a few miles, Princess Elizabeth said, "Zelda, I'm thirsty. Will you get me a drink?"

Zelda crossed her arms. "How can you rule a kingdom if you can't even get a drink of water?" Princess Elizabeth nodded and tried kneeling daintily by a stream, but she could not get close enough to drink. So she sprawled on the muddy bank of the stream and scooped water into her mouth.

As she drank, her mother's ring slid from her finger. Elizabeth did not notice that the ring had slipped off, but Zelda did.

Elizabeth stood up to brush the mud from her gown.

"Oh, no!" cried Elizabeth. "My mother's ring!"

Zelda held up the ring. "Is this what you're looking for?"

"Thank goodness! Zelda, you've saved me," said Elizabeth.

"This time, perhaps." Zelda slid the ring onto her own finger. "But what about next time? And after what just happened with the ring, I should take care of all your things. I'll ride Falada and keep an eye on your possessions."

Falada tried to warn Elizabeth not to let Zelda near her things, but Elizabeth felt that Zelda was right.

After they switched clothes, Princess Elizabeth and Zelda set off again. Elizabeth clomped along on the mare. Zelda rode Falada.

At the castle, the king and prince were waiting.

"Show me to my room and send up some food," said Zelda. "I'm tired and hungry."

The king was surprised by Zelda's rudeness, but he said politely, "We are delighted that you've arrived safely, princess." He turned to Elizabeth and said, "We'll find a room for you near the stable."

"Thank you," said Elizabeth. "You're so kind. But you see, I'm Princess Elizabeth."

Zelda snorted and showed the king the royal ring. "This proves who I am. My mother gave it to me before we left."

The king sent Elizabeth off with the goose boy, Conrad. "You're the new goose girl," Conrad told her.

Each morning Elizabeth and Conrad led the geese to a grassy meadow. At night Elizabeth slept on a pile of straw in the barn.

Elizabeth asked the stable boy where he had taken Falada. The boy led Elizabeth to a pasture in the far corner of the kingdom.

"Falada!" called Elizabeth. "I've found you. How are you?"

"Fit," said Falada. "This is a fine, grassy pasture with room to run. I'm exactly where a horse should be. But you are not where a princess should be. Your mother would be heartbroken."

Elizabeth and Falada talked and talked. Now that she had found her horse, Elizabeth insisted that she and Conrad take the geese to his pasture each day.

Conrad became annoyed. He was tired of trudging out to the far pasture. He went to the palace to complain to the king.

Conrad told the king about how Elizabeth talks to Falada.

"The horse talks?" asked the king.

"Yes." Conrad rolled his eyes. "He tells her how brokenhearted the queen would be to see her daughter tending geese."

The next morning, the king went to Falada's pasture and hid behind the fence. Soon Conrad and Elizabeth arrived with the geese. Falada galloped to the fence to greet Elizabeth.

"Tending geese is no job for a princess," Falada said to her.

The king heard this and nodded. "Conrad spoke the truth. The goose girl is the true Princess Elizabeth."

That night the king called for Zelda and Elizabeth. "You're a clever girl," he told Zelda. "Perhaps you can help me. A waiting woman has tried to pass herself off as a princess. Do you think forcing this girl to tend geese is the proper punishment?"

"No, your majesty," said Zelda. "She belongs in the stable, cleaning up after the horses."

The king nodded. "You're quite right." He plucked the queen's ring from Zelda's hand. "And that is exactly where you shall go."

As the guards dragged Zelda to the stables, the king slipped the ring onto Elizabeth's finger. "My deepest apologies," he told her.

Elizabeth and the prince were married the next day!

Baby Bluebird

Written by Lisa Harkrader
Illustrated by Cristina Ong

Baby Bluebird looked up at the sky. She watched all the other birds flying. "It's spring," she said. "I should be flying, but I don't know how to start."

Her friend Rabbit watched the birds, too.

"Flying looks a lot like hopping," said Rabbit. "In fact, I see birds hopping about all the time. Practice hopping with me. If you hop high enough, you might start to fly."

Rabbit hopped off through the garden. Baby Bluebird hopped after her. She was in the air, but soon came back down to the ground. Baby Bluebird tried again and again.

"What do you think, Baby Bluebird?" asked Rabbit. "Do you think hopping is like flying?"

"It's a little like flying," she said. "But I keep landing. I don't think real flying is so bouncy."

Baby Bluebird sat down in the pasture. She watched the other birds as they hopped and lifted off the ground.

Her friend Gopher watched the birds, too.

"It seems to me," said Gopher, "that flying is a lot like digging. Maybe if you practice digging with me, it will help you learn to flap your wings and fly. And digging is so much fun!"

"It doesn't look like much fun to me," said Baby Bluebird, "but I'll give it a try."

Baby Bluebird found a nice big patch of dirt. She flapped her wings on the ground, trying to dig a hole. But the dirt was too hard, and her feathers were too soft.

All her flapping didn't help Baby Bluebird fly, but it did raise a huge cloud of dust. Baby Bluebird coughed and sneezed.

"Maybe digging isn't like flying after all," she said. "I don't think flying is so sneezy."

Baby Bluebird fluttered her wings to get the dust out of her feathers. She sat down in the grass and looked at the birds taking off.

The birds hopped off the ground, then quickly flapped their wings. They flew as the breeze gently carried them through the air.

"What is their secret?" Baby Bluebird wondered as the birds flew over her. "I can hop. I can flap my wings. But I still can't fly."

Her friend Turtle watched the birds, too.

"Flying looks a little like swimming," he said. "Maybe if you practice swimming through the water with me, it will help you learn to glide through the air when you fly."

Baby Bluebird watched Turtle glide around the farm pond. "That doesn't look so hard," she said.

She plunged into the water. "Oh, my! It's so wet!" she cried.

"Paddle out here to the middle," said Turtle.

Baby Bluebird tried to paddle. She splashed and sputtered. Baby Bluebird wanted to glide like Turtle. But she could not. She just got wetter and wetter.

"Maybe swimming isn't like flying after all," she said. "I don't think flying is so soggy."

Baby Bluebird pulled herself onto the grassy edge of the pond. She fluttered her wings to dry them.

When her wings were dry, Baby Bluebird went to the cozy farmhouse and found Cat and Dog curled up on the porch. Baby Bluebird sat down beside them and watched the birds flying above her.

The birds playfully swooped through the sky. As they flew, they even sang a pretty song.

"These birds can fly *and* sing," said Baby Bluebird.

Cat and Dog watched and heard the birds, too.

"They look happy," said Cat.

"We sing when we're happy," said Dog.

"Maybe singing is part of flying," said Cat. "If you sing loud enough and long enough, maybe you'll begin to fly, too. We'll help you."

Dog howled. Cat yowled. Baby Bluebird tweeted. Then she twittered. She cheeped and chirped. She took a deep breath and let out a squawk! But nobody started to fly. Not Dog. Not Cat. Not Baby Bluebird.

"It's no use," said Baby Bluebird. "Singing won't make me fly. I might as well stop trying."

"Thank goodness," said Dog. "I don't have any howls left."

"Stop trying?" said Cat. "You can't stop trying. If you want to fly, you must find a way."

Baby Bluebird sat down on the porch steps and put her head in her wings. Suddenly, she looked up.

"Singing wasn't enough. And neither was hopping or flapping or gliding," she said. "But I think I know what I need to do."

Baby Bluebird took a running start. She hopped like Rabbit. She flapped her wings like Gopher. Once she was in the air, she glided like Turtle and the other birds through the beautiful sky.

"I'm flying!" she chirped.

Baby Bluebird swooped through the clouds. She flitted from tree to tree. Then Baby Bluebird lifted her head and, like Cat and Dog, began to sing.

The Lion and the Mouse

Adapted by Sarah Toast
Illustrated by Krista Brauckmann-Towns

One day a lion was taking a nice nap in the warm sun. Nearby, a busy little mouse scurried about looking for berries, but all the berries were too high for her to reach. Then the mouse spotted a lovely bunch of berries that she could reach by climbing the rock below them. When she did, the mouse discovered that she hadn't climbed a rock at all. She had climbed right on top of the lion's head!

The lion did not like to be bothered while he was sleeping. He awoke with a loud grumble. "Who dares to tickle my head while I'm taking a nap?" roared the lion.

The mouse could see how angry the lion was with her, so she jumped off his head and started to run away. The lion grabbed for the little mouse as quickly as he could, but she was too quick and he just missed her.

The quick little mouse hurried to get away from the lion. She zigged and zagged through the grass, but the lion was always just one step behind. At last the lion chased the mouse right back to where they had started. The poor little mouse was too tired to run anymore, and the lion scooped her up in his huge paw.

"Little mouse," roared the lion. "Don't you know that I am the king of the forest? Why did you wake me up from my pleasant nap by tickling my head?"

"Oh, please, lion," said the mouse. "I was only trying to get some lovely berries."

"Just see how much you like it when I tickle your head with my big claws," said the lion.

"Please, lion," pleaded the mouse. "If you spare me, I am sure I will be able to help you someday."

The lion stopped suddenly and looked at the mouse.

Then the lion began to smile. Then he began to laugh.

"How could you, a tiny mouse, help the most powerful animal in the forest?" he chuckled loudly. "That's so funny. I'll let you go—this time."

Then the lion laughed some more. He rolled over on his back, kicking and roaring with laughter. The mouse had to leap out of his way to avoid being crushed. Off she ran.

Still chuckling, the lion got up and realized he was hungry. He set out to find some lunch, and it wasn't long before he smelled food. Walking toward the good smell, the lion got caught in a trap set by hunters.

The lion was stuck in the strong ropes and the more the lion wriggled and struggled, the tighter the ropes held him. Fearing the hunters would soon return, the terrified lion roared for help.

The mouse heard the lion's roars from far away. At first she was a little afraid to go back, thinking the lion might hurt her. But the lion's cries for help made the mouse sad, and she remembered the promise she made to help him. The mouse hurried to where the lion was tangled in the trap.

"Oh, lion," said the mouse. "I know what it feels like to be caught. But you don't need to worry. I'll try to help you."

"I don't think there's anything you can do," said the lion. "These ropes are very strong. I've pushed and pulled with all my might, but I can't get free."

Suddenly the mouse said, "I have an idea! Just hold still, and I'll get to work." She quickly began chewing through the thick ropes with her small, sharp teeth. She worked and worked, and before long, the mouse had chewed through enough rope for the lion to get out of the trap!

Soon the lion wriggled out of the trap. He was very grateful to the mouse. "Mouse," he said, "I thank you for saving me, and I am sorry that I laughed at you before."

"I told you that I would help you someday when you agreed to spare me," said the mouse. "I always keep my word."

Then the lion scooped up the mouse and placed her on his head. He carried her back to the berry bush and lay down under it. "Mouse," he said, "I want you to reach up and pick one of those berries that you wanted earlier today."

The mouse plucked the biggest berry she could find. The lion took the mouse off of his head and held her in his paw. "Let's stick together," he said. "I can help you reach the berries, and you can get me out of a tight spot now and then."

"Okay!" said the mouse. "I can even pick you some berries to eat, and we can have a picnic together."

"I don't know if I would like to eat berries, but just having your company would be fine with me," said the lion.

And that is how the lion and the mouse became best friends. So if you are ever walking through the forest and see a lion laughing and carrying a little mouse, you will know that these two have become great friends because each displayed kindness to one another. Each vowed to take care of the other and to be there in a time of need. They have been friends ever since.

Playground Fun

Written by Sarah Toast
Illustrated by Joe Veno

Maria's dad is taking Maria and her two best friends to the new city park for the whole day. Maria and her dad pack lunch in a picnic basket. They bring along everything they'll need. They remember to bring a blanket to sit on and a kite for fun.

Nick and Nora are waiting at the entrance to the park when they arrive. "Hurry, Maria!" calls Nora. "There's so much to do!"

"Let's go to the playground first," says Nick.

"Here I come!" calls Maria.

The three friends are off and running toward the playground.

First they head for Fort Fun. There are children playing and laughing everywhere. Nick climbs a tall post all the way to the top. Nora balances on the tunnels. Maria waits for her turn on the rope swing.

"Look how tall I am!" shouts Nick.

"I'm balancing on a surfboard," says Nora.

"I'm swinging across a swamp filled with crocodiles," says Maria. "I hope they don't bite my feet!"

Then the three friends try the slide, swings, and teeter-totter.

"This is so much fun!" says Nick.

"This is the best playground ever!" says Nora.

Maria agrees, but she is laughing so hard that she cannot say anything. Then they all start to laugh together.

Nick, Nora, and Maria decide to go back to Fort Fun to climb and swing some more. Maria's dad looks for a picnic spot.

"Be careful," calls Maria's dad. "I'll be right over here looking for a good place to have lunch."

"We will!" they say. Then Nick, Nora, and Maria play follow the leader through Fort Fun!

Next Maria's dad suggests going over to the duck pond. "I think you'll like it very much," he says. "It is very pretty."

Everyone kneels at the edge of the pond to watch the mother duck and her three ducklings.

"Those little ducks can swim so well," says Nora.

"Yeah, and they are so small," says Nick. "I couldn't swim when I was just a baby!"

Maria sees a frog and a turtle among the cattails growing in the pond. "It is nice that these animals have a good home in the city," she says.

"Can you hop like a frog?" asks Maria's dad.

"Sure!" say Maria, Nick, and Nora. Then they all begin to hop around the pond.

"Ribbit! Ribbit!" says Nick.

This gives the friends an idea. They decide to play leapfrog across the park.

"Do you want to play, Dad?" asks Maria.

"I think my hopping days are over," laughs Maria's dad.

They all laugh as they hop across the grass.

When Nick, Nora, and Maria are tired of hopping, they lie down on the grass and look up at the sky.

"Now let's go to a different kind of pond," says Maria's dad.

"Yeah! Let's go!" say Nick, Nora, and Maria together. The children get up and dash to the wading pool. In the middle of the wading pool is a stone fountain spouting water.

Maria's dad takes off his shoes to wade in the water with Maria, Nick, and Nora.

"You look just like a big kid, Dad!" grins Maria. Maria's dad just smiles.

"Dolphins are my favorite animal," says Nora. She points to the statues of dolphins in the middle of the wading pool.

"They are very smart animals, too," says Nick.

"Let's pretend that we are dolphins swimming in the water," says Maria.

Nick, Nora, and Maria jump and splash in the wading pool.

"Don't get too wet," says Maria's dad. The three children stop splashing. They are through being dolphins for the day.

"That was fun!" says Maria.

"Let's go see more animals," says Nora. "Real animals, not statues." She leads the way to the petting zoo.

The children feed some cows and baby goats, and they even get to see a llama up close. They wish they could stay longer, but Nick's tummy starts growling.

"You sound like you have a lion in your tummy, Nick!" says Maria's dad.

"I'm getting sort of hungry," says Nick.

"So are we!" says everyone else at once. They pick a nice spot for lunch. Nora spreads the blanket. Nick sets out the tasty sandwiches. Maria pours the juice, and her dad puts the fruit on a plate for everyone to share.

While they are eating lunch, Maria says, "Everywhere we've gone in the park today, I've seen a bluebird gathering little twigs and leaves."

"Keep your eyes peeled," says her dad. "Maybe you'll see the nest she is making."

"That would be exciting!" says Nora.

Everyone finishes eating and helps to throw away the trash.

After they tidy up the picnic area, Maria leaves a bread crust for the busy bluebird. "Who would like to play a game of baseball?" she asks. "I heard there's a baseball diamond here."

They get to the diamond just as a game begins. Maria, Nick, and Nora have fun playing on different teams. Nick turns out to be a pretty good pitcher. Nora makes a home run. Maria catches a high fly ball.

After a few innings, everyone decides to switch teams. They do not keep score as they play, and everyone stays up to bat until they hit the ball.

"This is so much fun!" says Nora.

"I'm ready for the big league now," says Nick, kicking up the dust around the diamond.

Maria just giggles. Then they see the bluebird fly by, carrying some twigs.

"Look! There's the bird!" says Maria's dad.

They try to see where the bird is flying off to, but it disappears amongst the trees.

"Well, we'll just have to keep looking," says Maria.

They all begin walking away from the baseball game, keeping their eyes open for the bluebird. Beyond the baseball diamond is a hill. It is breezy on the hilltop and there aren't many trees. It is the perfect place to fly kites.

"Let's go fly kites!" says Nora.

Park workers are handing kites to all the kids. The workers show how to let out the string so their kites can fly higher and higher in the sky. They explain how tails keep their kites from spinning around and crashing to the ground.

Maria and her dad brought a kite from home. While Nick and Nora learn from the park workers, Maria and her dad try flying their own kite.

Soon everyone has a kite in the air! The sky is decorated with lots of pretty colors and designs. Children are laughing as they run, trying to keep their kites in the sky.

Suddenly they see the bluebird gathering more twigs. Maria, Nick, and Nora try to follow the bird once again, but their kite strings get tangled. They lose the bird as it flies between the colorful kites.

From the hilltop, Maria, Nick, and Nora can see many people gathering below to watch a show.

"Let's go watch," says Nick. They hurry so they can get a good spot in the grass.

When they get there and sit down, a man is setting up a little puppet theater. He blows on a horn to start the show. Then he makes his puppets perform a funny play.

After the play, Maria's dad gathers all of their belongings. The children relax in the grass before heading home.

"We had a busy day, but not as busy as the bluebird's," says Maria. "Look! Her nest is in this tree!"

"And look!" says Nora. "There are eggs in her nest."

"Wow! It is the first new nest in our new park," says Nick.

After watching the bluebird sit on her nest for a while, they all get ready to go home.

"What should we do tomorrow?" asks Maria.

"I don't know. How about a picnic in the park?" say Nick and Nora. What a great idea!

The Little Dutch Boy

Adapted by Sarah Toast
Illustrated by Linda Dockey Graves

Long ago there was a boy named Hans who lived with his mother in a pretty town in Holland. The land of Holland is very flat, and much of it is below the level of the sea. The farmers there built big walls called dikes to keep the sea from flooding their farms.

One day Hans's mother packed a basket of fruit, bread, and cheese for Hans to take to their old friend, Mr. Van Notten. Mr. Van Notten lived outside of town, and it was a long way to his house. As Hans set out, his mother told him not to stay too late. She wanted him to be home before dark.

Mr. Van Notten had only an old dog to keep him company, so he was very happy when Hans came to visit him. To get to Mr. Van Notten's home, Hans just followed the main road out of town. The road ran right alongside the dike.

Hans was very thirsty and hungry after his long walk, so Mr. Van Notten made cocoa and set out the bread and cheese. After their meal, the boy and the old man talked by the fire. Hans enjoyed Mr. Van Notten's stories of the olden days.

When Mr. Van Notten's dog scratched at the door to be let out, Hans noticed that the sky had become dark and stormy. He decided that he should leave right away to get home before it started to rain. Hans said good-bye to Mr. Van Notten and promised to come back soon.

Hans walked quickly, but he was not even halfway home when the air became much colder and the wind began to blow. It wasn't long before cold, stinging raindrops battered Hans as he struggled against the powerful wind. The weather made it difficult for Hans to walk, but he kept going. "If I just keep putting one foot in front of the other," said Hans to himself, "I'll be home soon."

The strong wind made the trees bend low, and it flattened the flowers. Hans was getting cold, and he had to hold his hat on his head to keep it from blowing away. I hope my mother isn't upset when I arrive home so cold and wet, he thought.

Hans was getting more and more tired with every step, but he had to keep going. He remembered that his mother wanted him home before dark, and Hans did not want to let her down. He wanted to get home so she would not worry.

"I promised that I would be home before dark," Hans kept saying to himself. His teeth began to chatter.

Hans kept his head down against the wind as he trudged along the road. It was so dark outside that Hans had no idea he was nearing the town until he lifted his head for a moment. Hans was happy to see the dike right in front of him. It meant he would soon be home and out of the rain.

"Oh, thank goodness!" said Hans. "I'm almost there."

Hans had never been so happy to see the dike before. It was the only familiar thing he had seen since he left Mr. Van Notten's house and the rain started.

Even with all the raindrops falling and dripping from the trees, Hans noticed some water where it should not have been. There was a small hole in the dike, and a trickle of water was seeping through the stones.

Hans knew that the storm must have whipped up the waves of the sea, and the weight of the water had made a crack in the dike. Even the stone wall was no match for this horrible storm.

I've got to warn everybody that the dike has sprung a leak! thought Hans.

Hans began to run. The wind was still blowing against him and he felt as though his legs might blow out from underneath him with each step he took.

"I must get to the town! The town is in danger!" Hans told himself as he ran.

It seemed to Hans that he had been running for a very long time. He knew the town must be very close. It was hard to see where he was going in the darkness and pouring rain.

Finally, when Hans lifted his head again, he saw the town. It did not look the same, though. It looked very dark and empty.

Hans ran into town. "The dike is breaking!" he shouted. "Help! We've got to fix the dike!"

Shout as he would, no one heard Hans. Nobody else was outside, and all the houses had been completely shut because of the storm. All the doors were secured tightly and bolted, every window closed and shuttered.

Hans soon realized his shouting was not doing any good. He stopped running to catch his breath. Leaning against a fence, Hans tried to think of what he should do next.

Hans knew his mother must be worrying about him, but he also knew that the tiny hole in the dike was getting bigger every minute. If the hole got big enough, the sea would surely push its way through and break the dike. If the dike broke, all would be lost. The sea would flood the farms and wash away the pretty little town.

"Somebody help!" shouted Hans once more. But nobody answered. Hans kept thinking about the dike. He did not want the town to be washed away. But he did not know what one small boy could do to save the town. Then he had an idea.

As fast as he could, Hans ran back to the place where he had seen the water seeping through the dike. Sure enough, the crack was bigger now than when he first had spotted it. Hans knew that the crack must be fixed soon. Otherwise the sea would break through, and it would be too late. There was nothing else to do, so Hans balled up his fist and pushed it into the hole to stop the little stream of water.

Hans was proud and happy that one small boy could hold back the sea. He was sure that his worried mother would soon send people to look for him. But minutes turned into hours as Hans patiently stood there.

As darkness fell, Hans became very cold and tired, and his arm began to ache. He had to force himself to keep standing on his tired legs. To keep himself going, Hans thought about how important it was to hold back the water of the sea.

As Hans stood in the cold rain by the dike, he thought about the warmth of the fireplace at home. Then he thought about how good it was going to feel to lie down in his snug bed. These thoughts helped the exhausted boy get through the long night.

When Hans didn't come home that evening, his mother began to worry. Even while the rain was falling, she kept looking out the door for Hans to come back. At last she decided that Hans must have waited out the storm at Mr. Van Notten's. She thought he must have spent the night there because it was too dark to come home after the storm.

After looking out the door one more time, Hans's mother closed up the house and went to bed, but she couldn't sleep. She was too worried about her little boy.

"Hans, where are you?" said Hans's mother out loud. "Please be safe and warm and dry." She sat on the edge of her bed and clutched the bed covers tightly. She did not like the idea of her little boy out in the storm. If only she knew he was safe at Mr. Van Notten's, then she could rest easy.

It was a very long night for Hans's mother. Her heart was filled with worry.

Early the next morning, Mr. Van Notten decided to take a walk to Hans's home. He wanted to thank Hans for the visit and thank his mother for the tasty food.

When Mr. Van Notten came to where Hans was, the boy was trembling and cold. Hans's arm hurt from the effort of keeping his fist in the hole of the dike, and his legs were ready to collapse from standing all night.

Mr. Van Notten could not believe his eyes! He told Hans to hold firm for just a little while longer. Mr. Van Notten ran into town to get help.

"Don't worry, Hans," said Mr. Van Notten. "I'll be back in a jiffy. You're doing a great job, just hang on a little longer." Soon Mr. Van Notten returned with someone to take care of Hans and materials to repair the dike.

Hans was wrapped in blankets and carried home. His mother was so happy to see him, but she was frightened by the state he was in. He was put to bed and given warm broth to drink. His mother rubbed his fingers and his stiff legs.

The town doctor came by the house to check on Hans. Hans was all right, he had just gotten a little cold. Hans was so tired that he fell asleep right away and did not wake up until the following day.

Word quickly spread through the town of how Hans had held back the sea all by himself. The townspeople were very curious. They went to the dike to see the hole that Hans had bravely kept plugged with his tiny fist.

As soon as Hans felt strong enough, he and his mother went back to the dike to see the repairs that were being made.

Everyone in town was overjoyed to see Hans. They thanked him for holding back the mighty sea and for saving them from what would have otherwise been a terrible flood.

The mayor of the town presented Hans with a medal to honor his dedication, and all the townspeople cheered loudly. Hans would forever after be remembered as a hero.

Years later, even after Hans was all grown up, people still called him the little boy with the big heart.

Counting Sheep

Written by Brian Conway
Illustrated by Kathy Wilburn

Fleecy was a young lamb who was full of energy. She romped through the meadows every day. And she could run and play all day long.

The crickets and butterflies let her chase them through the fields. None of the other sheep could keep up with the insects. But pouncing, prancing Fleecy surely could. She never wore out.

At the end of the day, Fleecy's friends would fly away. Fleecy wished she could fly like the crickets and butterflies. She saw the sky as a wonderful, magical place. Fleecy spent each night staring at it and dreaming.

Fleecy really thought that someday she might take to the sky and fly. The lively little lamb got so wrapped up in her thoughts some nights that she was just about ready to jump right out of her fleece and up to the stars. Fleecy had so much energy that she stayed awake even when it was time to sleep.

Fleecy's mother began to worry about her. "It's not good for a little lamb to stay up so late," her mother told her one night. "A growing lamb needs her sleep."

"I'd like to dream and be awake at the same time, Mom," Fleecy said.

Fleecy's mother had an idea. She knew of Fleecy's fondness for the sky. "Look up to the sky," she said, "and count the stars you see. I'm sure you'll fall asleep soon."

Fleecy gazed at the bright stars in the night sky. She imagined she was high above the field, flying among them. In her dream, she sailed from star to brilliant star, tapping each one as she counted it.

"One, two, three," Fleecy counted. She only got to three before she slipped into sleep.

Fleecy's mother was right. Fleecy slept so well that she had more energy than ever the next day.

"I flew higher than a butterfly in my dream last night," she told her butterfly friends as she chased them through the field. "I even touched the stars!"

That night, when it was time for sleep, there were no stars to count. Fleecy was very disappointed. She had hoped to fly in her dreams and touch many more stars this time.

Again, Fleecy could not sleep. Even after a busy day with the butterflies, Fleecy was still full of energy.

Fleecy's mother noticed the little lamb's restlessness. "Perhaps you should try counting the clouds tonight, dear," said Fleecy's mother. "That should help you get to sleep."

Fleecy watched the clouds slowly crossing the night sky. She imagined that she was with them, high above the field. In her dream, she jumped and flew from cloud to cloud. To Fleecy, every cloud was a soft pillow that wrapped gently around her.

"One, two, three," she counted, as she hopped among the clouds. Fleecy only got to three before she was fast asleep.

Sure enough, Fleecy's mother was right again! Counting the clouds really did help Fleecy fall asleep. Once again Fleecy was full of energy for another busy day. She jumped and ran and played through the meadow.

"Last night I hopped from cloud to cloud," Fleecy told her friends in the meadow. "Tonight I'll fly to the clouds at the very tippety-top of the sky!"

But the next night there were no clouds. There weren't any stars, either.

"How will I get to sleep now?" Fleecy asked her mother.

Fleecy's mother thought for a moment, then she said, "Try counting the sheep. We'll always be here."

Fleecy started counting all the sheep sleeping in the field. She imagined floating high above the field, and the sleeping sheep rose up with her as she counted them. In her dream, every sheep's white woolly coat was a puffy cloud in the dark night sky.

"One, two, three," she counted as she floated.

Fleecy only got to three before she was sleeping soundly, just like the rest of the sheep.

From then on, Fleecy's mother never had to worry about her restlessness. That is because Fleecy counted sheep every night. She imagined that she was a woolly cloud rising up to the sky, and she counted as the other sheep rose from the field to join her in her dream.

"One, two, three," she counted as she dozed off.

Each night Fleecy only got to three before she was fast asleep. She always slept well, dreaming that she was floating restfully among the soft, puffy clouds.

And Fleecy always had lots of energy in the daytime, too. "I floated to the tippety-top of the sky last night," she told the insects while she chased them around the meadow. "And someday I will fly just like you!"

Though she tried again and again, Fleecy was never able to fly like her friends did. But in her starry dreams she came closer to flying than any little lamb had ever known.

Farm Day

Written by Sarah Toast
Illustrated by Joe Veno

"Katie! We're so glad to see you," says Aunt Sally. "So many new animals have come to live on the farm that we haven't had time to name them."

"We're counting on you. You always think up the best names," says Uncle Peter.

As soon as Dad unloads her suitcases from the car and says good-bye, Katie is ready to get started.

"Let's hurry to the barn and say good morning to your new cow," says Katie. "Brownie is a good name for a cow."

"What a nice name," says Aunt Sally. "Let's meet her."

In the milking barn, Aunt Sally sits on a low stool and begins to milk the new cow.

"Mooo," says the cow.

"Brownie is not a brown cow," says Katie. "I guess that means there won't be any chocolate milk."

"All cows give white milk," says Uncle Peter. "The milk you buy at the store comes from cows just like this one."

Aunt Sally shows Katie how the cow gives milk. "It doesn't hurt her," she says. She fills a pail with milk, a little bit at a time.

"I think Spots would be a good name for this cow," says Katie.

"Mooo," says Spots.

"I think she likes that name," says Uncle Peter. "I knew you would be good at this!"

Katie pats the cow as Aunt Sally continues to milk her. Spots is calm as Aunt Sally fills the pail to the rim.

"Thank you, Spots," says Aunt Sally. Spots just swishes her tail back and forth.

"I think that means 'You're welcome'," says Katie.

Uncle Peter and Aunt Sally laugh as they leave the barn.

Out in the barnyard, Uncle Peter feeds the chickens the corn and grains they like to eat. The chickens scratch at the dirt and peck at the grain. Katie thinks the little chicks are fun to watch as they bop up and down the barnyard.

"Listen to this little chick. He's trying to crow," says Katie.

"He's a baby rooster. Soon he'll wake us up at sunrise," says Uncle Peter.

"His name is Early Bird," says Katie.

"Peep-a-doodle-peep," says Early Bird.

"Will all these chicks grow up to be roosters?" asks Katie.

"No, the male chicks will become roosters. The female chicks will become hens and lay eggs," explains Uncle Peter.

"Oh, then I will name this female chick Eggy," says Katie.

"That's a wonderful name," says Uncle Peter.

Katie asks Uncle Peter if she can help to feed the chickens, too. He hands her the bucket of grain and lets her take a big handful.

"Now just sprinkle it lightly," says Uncle Peter. Katie sprinkles the grain along the barnyard, just as Uncle Peter said. "Very good, Katie! You are making these chickens very happy," he says.

The next stop for Katie and Uncle Peter is the horse barn. Aunt Sally is already there raking hay in the hayloft.

"Good morning, Pinto Bean," says Katie to the farm horse. He is an old friend. "We are going to clean your stall and give you some fresh hay to eat."

Katie goes up to the hayloft to help Aunt Sally with the hay. In the hayloft, Katie sees a barn cat that she has never seen before.

"Barn cats are not just pets. They have important work to do. They keep mice out of the barn," says Aunt Sally.

"I'll name this striped cat Tiger," says Katie. "And the cat who is helping Uncle Peter should be called Lion."

"Meow," says Tiger.

"Meow, meow," says Lion.

Katie gives a handful of hay to Pinto Bean. The horse chews loudly. Katie brushes Pinto Bean with a special horse brush while he munches on his hay.

Uncle Peter uses a pitchfork to clean the old hay out of Pinto Bean's stall. Pinto Bean nods his head up and down.

"Pinto Bean likes fresh hay," says Katie.

The next stop for the hard-working farmhands is the pig pen.

"I don't want to go in the muddy pig pen," Katie says as she climbs on the fence.

"Pigs are great," says Farmer Bob. "They're recyclers. I feed them leftovers, called slop, and they grow big." Farmer Bob helps out Uncle Peter and Aunt Sally with the chores on the farm. Farmer Bob knows a lot about animals.

"Mud keeps pigs' skin cool," says Uncle Peter. "Katie, you like swimming pools. Pigs like mud puddles."

"I'll call the little pig I'm scratching Mud Pie," says Katie.

"Oink," says Mud Pie.

"Mud Pie likes to have his back scratched," says Katie.

"Pigs are very smart animals, too," says Farmer Bob. "They make really great pets. But not many people can have pigs in their homes."

"I don't know about keeping a pig as a pet," says Katie. "I usually let my pets sleep on my bed."

Farmer Bob and Uncle Peter laugh. Katie laughs, too, thinking about all the mud she would get on her blankets.

After feeding the pigs, Katie's tummy starts to grumble. It is time for lunch!

"Let's go to the house," says Uncle Peter.

At the house, Katie and Uncle Peter wash up for lunch. They sit at a table in the yard next to the vegetable garden.

For lunch Katie eats a tasty sandwich made with lettuce and tomatoes from the garden. She drinks a glass of milk from Spots the cow. Everything is delicious!

Just then, a big dog runs into the yard and puts his paws on the picnic table.

"Who is he, Uncle Peter?" asks Katie.

"I don't know," says Uncle Peter.

The big dog sniffs the food on the table and runs away.

"That's a very silly dog," says Katie.

Katie is having a very nice time at the farm with Uncle Peter and Aunt Sally. She sees how much hard work goes into running a farm. She likes the fresh air and all the animals.

After she is finished eating, Katie helps clean up the lunch dishes and wipe down the table.

Uncle Peter needs to mend the fence around the cow pasture. Katie comes to watch. In the pasture, Katie sees the big, silly dog again. He runs over to her to play.

While her uncle pulls the fence wire tight, Katie tries to think of a name for the big dog.

"All the animals on the farm work, but this dog just wants to play," says Katie. "I'll call you Funny Bones."

"Woof, woof!" barks Funny Bones.

Katie and Funny Bones run around the pasture. Katie finds a stick and throws it for the dog. Funny Bones happily carries the stick back to Katie. Then Katie climbs a tree. Funny Bones thinks this is another game.

"Woof!" barks Funny Bones at Katie.

"You really are a silly dog!" laughs Katie. "Dogs can't climb trees. You have to stay down there."

Funny Bones barks again and runs around the tree. He does not stop barking until Katie comes down from the tree.

"I think Funny Bones thought I was going to fall," Katie tells Uncle Peter. "I guess he does work. He's a watchdog!"

In the farm workshop, Uncle Peter works on his tractor. A farmer knows how to fix all the machines on the farm.

"Your tractor has a name," says Katie. "I call it Green Machine because it plows the fields, plants, and harvests."

"Chug-a-rumble-rumble," goes Green Machine.

After working in the workshop, Uncle Peter and Farmer Bob put out grass for Spots and the other cows. Katie helps. She feeds grass to a young calf.

"I think her name should be Little Spots," says Katie.

"Mooo," says Little Spots.

"Little Spots says it is getting late," says Katie.

"We better get back to the house," says Uncle Peter. "It will be getting dark soon." Indeed, the sun is beginning to set. Fireflies can be seen twinkling here and there.

The farmers are tired after a busy day. Uncle Peter and Aunt Sally rest on the porch swing. But Katie still has one more job to do before bed.

"This firefly is called Starlight. This one is Star Bright. And this one's name is Good Night," says Katie.

Rapunzel

Adapted by Lisa Harkrader
Illustrated by Barbara Lanza

There was once a poor man who lived with his wife in a tiny cottage. They worked hard tending their garden, but their land was small, and the soil was rocky. They could grow barely enough food to feed themselves.

Their cottage stood next to a witch's castle. The castle's grounds were filled with lush gardens and orchards that grew more food than the witch could eat.

One day the poor, hungry man crept over the garden wall and filled his sack with peas and squash, potatoes, corn and tomatoes.

Just then a voice called, "Drop those vegetables!"

The man turned and saw the witch looming over him.

"You won't get away with stealing from me! When your first child is born, you must give the baby to me," said the witch.

A year went by, and a daughter was born to the man and his wife. They named her Rapunzel and kept her safely hidden in the cottage. The man read stories and played games with her. The woman made up lullabies and sang them to her night and day.

"You are the most precious child in the world," said Rapunzel's mother and father.

The witch watched the cottage from her castle. One day she heard the woman singing.

"Lullabies?" snarled the witch. The evil witch crept up to the cottage and peeked in the window. There she saw the baby Rapunzel. "A child!" shrieked the witch.

Before the man or woman could stop her, the witch snatched Rapunzel from her cradle.

The witch carried Rapunzel to her castle and locked her inside. The chambers were dark and lonely, but as the years went by Rapunzel grew into a lovely girl, well-mannered and bright.

Rapunzel was so bright, she began asking questions.

"Why are the windows covered so we can't see out?" asked Rapunzel. "What is beyond that big door?"

The witch would not reply, but she knew that Rapunzel would try to find her own answers to these questions. So she led Rapunzel to a tower deep in the woods. The tower had no doors and no stairs. The only opening was one small window high above the ground. The witch locked Rapunzel inside. Now poor Rapunzel did not even have the company of the witch. She looked out the tower window at the forest animals and imagined talking to them.

Each morning the witch brought food to Rapunzel. She called up, "Rapunzel, Rapunzel! Let down your hair."

Rapunzel would bend her head out the window and let her hair tumble down. It was so long that it reached the ground and so strong that the witch was able to climb up to the window.

Rapunzel was very lonely in the tower, so even the sight of the witch was comforting. Every day Rapunzel sang familiar lullabies to pass the time.

One day, a prince from a nearby kingdom heard Rapunzel singing and followed her voice to the tower.

The prince realized that the song was coming from inside, but he could not find a way in. He listened to the enchanting music, hoping to see whose voice filled the woods with song.

Then he saw the witch creeping through the woods. The prince heard her call out, "Rapunzel, Rapunzel! Let down your hair."

The prince watched in amazement as the shiny, golden locks dropped to the ground. "She is by far the most beautiful creature on earth," he said.

The prince waited until the witch was gone. Then, he called out, "Rapunzel, Rapunzel! Let down your hair."

Rapunzel let down her hair, expecting to see the witch again. When the prince climbed into view, Rapunzel gasped.

"Don't be afraid," said the kind prince. "I heard your beautiful lullabies and wanted to meet you."

Rapunzel was not afraid. Something about the prince's face was kind and gentle. The prince was the most handsome thing Rapunzel had ever seen. The two fell in love immediately.

"Would you like to leave this place?" asked the prince. "I'll help you—somehow."

Rapunzel was so excited at the thought of leaving the lonely tower. "My hair!" she said. "We can escape by using my long hair." Then Rapunzel let down her hair. The prince climbed down Rapunzel's hair, then caught her as she leaped to freedom. They set off for the prince's kingdom.

As they passed a small cottage, Rapunzel heard a familiar lullaby. "It's one of my lullabies!" said Rapunzel. They looked inside the cottage and saw a man and woman.

"Your songs are lovely," Rapunzel told the woman.

"I made them up for my daughter, Rapunzel," said the woman. "An evil witch took her when she was just a baby. She would be about your age now. I miss her so much."

Rapunzel hugged the man and woman. "I'm Rapunzel," she said. "I've escaped from the witch."

Rapunzel sang the lullabies in a full, joyful voice. "These songs have led me back to you," said Rapunzel.

They all sang the beautiful lullabies together.

The Steadfast Tin Soldier

Adapted by Bette Killion
Illustrated by Jim Salvati

Once upon a time, there were twenty-five tin soldiers in a wooden box. Each was brave. Each was handsome, and each wore a smart, blue uniform. One soldier, Will, had only a single leg. He had been made last, and the toy maker had run out of tin.

Will stood just as straight on his one leg as the others did on two, and he was just as brave and handsome.

The tin soldiers were given to a boy on his birthday. The boy was very happy with his soldiers. He liked Will, even though he had only one leg.

When the boy took out the soldiers to play with them, Will looked around and found that he was in a nursery. There were many other toys in the room. On the far side of the table, he saw a castle made of pink paper. In the doorway of the castle stood a beautiful paper maiden. Will fell in love with her at once.

The paper maiden, whose name was Alyssa, was a very graceful dancer. One arm was raised above her head, and one foot was lifted so high behind her that Will thought she had only one leg, just like him. She wore a dress made of sky blue gauze with a blue ribbon on one sleeve.

She would make a perfect wife for me, thought Will. He gazed and gazed at the paper maiden, unable to take his eyes off her. She was the most beautiful toy in the nursery.

When evening came, the boy put all the soldiers except Will back in the box. When it grew dark, the toys began to play together. The tin soldier stood stiffly at attention and watched Alyssa. She stood still and looked at him out of the corner of her eye. Will wanted to talk to her, but he could only stand and watch her as she danced.

The next morning the boy took the soldier and stood him on the windowsill. All of a sudden, a gust of wind blew. Will fell out of the window, and his hat stuck in the dirt between stones in the street below.

Soon it began to rain. The rain came down so hard that water ran in torrents down the street. Will bravely waited for the heavy downpour to end. When it was over, two boys found the toy soldier. They made a paper boat, put Will in it, and floated it down a canal.

Will had never been in a boat before. He was not scared, though. He thought the boat ride was quite peaceful. He calmly sailed down the canal.

As he continued to sail, he thought he must be getting further and further away from the nursery. He wondered if he would ever see the boy or Alyssa again.

Will tried to think good thoughts as he sailed. He looked at the passing scenery. There were so many things to look at that were different than the nursery. But no matter how much he liked the scenes around him, he longed for home.

The canal emptied into a dark tunnel. The waters were so swift that the paper boat whirled and tipped dangerously, but the tin soldier held fast and was very brave. How he wished that the beautiful Alyssa could be here with him! That would make him the happiest.

A big rat who lived in the tunnel suddenly loomed up beside the paper boat.

"Where is your pass?" the rat demanded. "Give me your pass at once or you won't get by."

The tin soldier remained still and steady. The rat swam as fast as he could, but the boat whirled away too quickly in the current.

Soon the rat was left behind. Will could hear the sound of the rat's voice fading as the boat whirled on. He let out a great sigh of relief.

Will wondered what was in store for him next and if he would ever see the beautiful Alyssa again. The current grew stronger and stronger, pulling the boat along faster and faster. Just as Will began to see daylight at the end of the tunnel, he heard a terrible splashing. Will's boat was heading straight for a waterfall!

Will knew that the poor, soggy boat could never survive a waterfall, but there was no avoiding it. He pulled himself up and stood more bravely than ever on his one leg.

Once the soggy paper boat was caught in the rushing waterfall, it quickly filled with water and sank.

The water was very cold. Will could not swim, especially with just one leg.

"This must certainly be my end," said the tin soldier as he plunged swiftly down into the whirlpool. "I will never again see the beautiful Alyssa, nor will I ever know how wonderful it would have been to watch her dance for me."

Round and round he whirled. As he spun around, he imagined Alyssa spinning in her beautiful blue dress. He saw her lovely face over and over again. I wish she knew that she was on my mind until the very end, Will thought.

Just then, Will's shiny blue uniform caught the eye of a large fish. The fish was quite hungry. It stopped, looked Will over from head to toe, and then swallowed him in one gulp. It must have thought that Will was a shiny minnow.

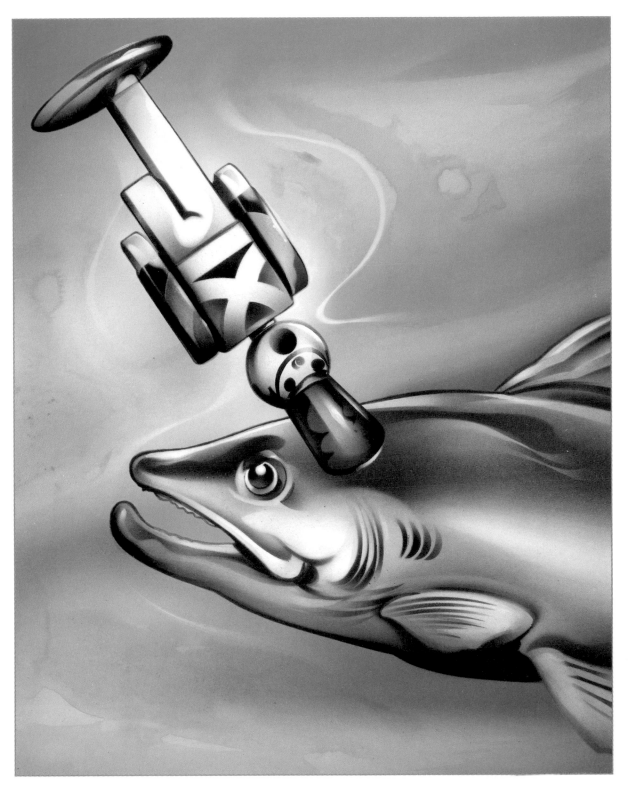

It was much darker in the fish than in the tunnel, but Will held himself as straight as he could. The fish seemed to dash around frantically for a time and then lay quiet. It was very still.

After a long time there was a flash like lightning, and Will saw daylight again. The fish had been caught on someone's hook. Now it was in a kitchen, and the cook was preparing it for dinner.

"My goodness! Look at this tin soldier inside my fish!" exclaimed the cook. She pulled Will out, then wiped him off and brought him to the nursery.

Will looked around and saw the box where his brothers lived and the maiden's paper castle. His heart started to beat faster because he realized that he was home. The boy came into the nursery and looked at the tin soldier.

"Where have you been?" the little boy asked him. "You're damp and smell like a fish."

Suddenly he opened the window and tossed Will into the flower garden below. Will lay among the petunias and felt sad, but he remained brave.

Just then, a gentle wind blew over him. It blew through the house, picked up Alyssa, and blew her straight out the open window and into the garden.

With a graceful little flutter, the paper dancer landed next to Will among the petunias. The two looked at each other with beating hearts and adoring eyes. Then the two toys stood close together.

"Will you stay with me and be my wife?" Will asked.

"Yes, forever and ever!" she whispered.

And that is exactly what Alyssa did. Will and Alyssa were married beneath the leaves of a low-growing plant. Sometimes, when the moon shone through the branches above and the air was balmy and warm, the graceful Alyssa would dance for her husband.

She always remained true to Will, as did the steadfast tin soldier to her.

I Like School

Written by Sarah Toast
Illustrated by Steve Henry

This is Jake's first day of school. He feels happy and scared at the same time. He is happy because he knows he will see his friends and he has heard that school is fun. But he is scared because he does not know his teacher and he might miss his mom.

Jake's mom takes him to the classroom and says hello to the teacher, Miss Martin. Miss Martin is nice. She even says hello to Jake's stuffed dog Snarf. Snarf has come along to keep Jake company on his first day of school.

"Snarf is shy," Jake tells Miss Martin.

Jake kisses his mom good-bye and takes a look around the classroom. It looks like a pretty interesting place.

"Jake, why don't you find the cubby with your name on it," says Miss Martin. "You can put your backpack in there. You may even find a little surprise."

Jake finds his very own cubby. He likes to see his name on the sign. He feels grown-up. Jake's welcome-to-school surprise is an eraser shaped like a funny dinosaur.

"Thank you, Miss Martin," says Jake. He puts his new dinosaur eraser in his pocket.

Jake is not feeling so nervous anymore. Children are still arriving to the classroom carrying their backpacks and special things from home. Jake is glad he wasn't the last one to arrive.

Jake looks at the little girl next to him. She looks a little scared. Jake asks her what surprise present she got in her cubby hole. The girl smiles.

"I got an eraser shaped like a blue dog!" she says. "My name is Judy. What's your name?"

"My name is Jake," he says. Jake thinks Judy is nice.

When everyone has arrived, Miss Martin says, "Please sit in a chair at one of the tables." The chairs and tables are just the right size for children.

Jake says hello to three of his pals. He doesn't know the rest of the children. He sees Judy sitting at his table.

Miss Martin asks them to say their names for the rest of the class. This makes Jake feel scared. He does not like talking in front of people he does not know. But after he sees a few children stand up and say their names, he does not feel so scared. When it is his turn to say his name, Jake stands up tall and speaks clearly. He looks at Judy, and she smiles at him.

Miss Martin tells the class all about herself. Jake is happy to know that she has a dog. Snarf is happy to know that, too.

Then Miss Martin teaches the class a Good Morning song. The whole class sings,

> Good morning to you!
>
> > Good morning to you!
>
> Good morning, dear teacher.
>
> > Good morning to you!

Everyone gets a classroom job to do for a week. This week, Jake will feed the fish with his friend Mark.

Mark has a fish at home. He says, "You can feed the fish first, Jake. I do it all the time."

Mark shows Jake how much food to sprinkle into the water. "It isn't good to feed fish too much food. It could make them sick," says Mark.

Some more of the classroom jobs are to water the plants and straighten the books on the bookshelves. Some children hand out papers, crayons, and scissors. Others help Miss Martin decorate a bulletin board with leaves made out of construction paper.

Mark thinks all of these jobs sound like fun, not work. He can't wait to try each one. He likes the fish a lot. Mark is nice for teaching him about fish and for letting him feed them first.

So far, school has been great. Jake is glad that he has friends in his class. But everyone seems so friendly, Jake has a feeling that he would be just fine even if he did not know anyone.

Jake and Mark watch the fish for a while after they feed them. It is fun to watch them dart around, picking up the food.

When all the classroom jobs are finished, Miss Martin says, "Line up! It is time for recess."

The class lines up shortest to tallest. The tallest stand in the back of the line. The shortest get to stand in the front. Jake stands in the middle.

Then Miss Martin leads the class to the playground that is right outside the school.

First, Jake plays in the sandbox with a boy and girl he has just met. There are shovels and pails and all sorts of toys to play with. Jake makes a castle and uses a gum wrapper for a flag on top. He is proud of the way his castle looks.

After Jake is finished playing in the sand, he takes a turn on the swings with his friend from across the street. They see who can swing the highest.

"Boys! Not too high, now!" calls Miss Martin from the school doorway. Jake was happy that Miss Martin told them to stop swinging so high. He was getting a little nervous being so high up. The boys put their feet down to slow down their swings.

"That was fun!" says Jake.

Miss Martin calls for everyone to line up again when recess is over. She leads the class back to the room and says, "It is time for a snack. Please find your seat."

Jake is hungry! Some helpers pass out cookies, fruit, and little cartons of cold milk. The boys and girls get to know each other while they eat their snacks.

After snacks, Miss Martin asks the class to join her in the art corner for finger painting. Mrs. Wiggins is the art teacher. She tells everyone to be creative.

Jake spreads paint on wet paper with his hands and makes squiggles with his fingers. It feels squishy and slippery.

"Nice job, Jake," says Miss Martin.

"Thank you, Miss Martin," says Jake.

Jake likes to paint. It is one of his favorite things to do at home. He is surprised that he gets to paint at school. It makes him very happy.

Jake looks at what the other children are painting. Many of the children paint pictures of their pets or their houses. Jake thinks that is nice. He can't wait to show his mom his painting.

After a while, the children hang their paintings to dry. They all wash their hands and hang up their smocks to dry, too. Miss Martin asks, "Who wants to hear a good story?"

The children raise their hands and say, "We do!" Everyone follows Miss Martin to the story rug. This is a time to get very comfortable and listen quietly while Miss Martin reads. Some children go to the play area to find a stuffed toy to cuddle with. Jake brings Snarf to the story rug. Snarf loves story time!

Today's story is about a tugboat and a steamship. Miss Martin has a great story-telling voice. She uses different voices for the tugboat and the steamship. Jake thinks this is funny. Miss Martin never forgets to show the pictures.

Jake gets a little sleepy as he listens to Miss Martin's voice. He can tell that Snarf is sleepy, too.

"Stay awake, Snarf," says Jake quietly. "The good part of the story is coming up!"

Jake and Snarf stay awake until the end of the story. Jake can hear one boy breathing very heavily. He giggles because he thinks this boy is asleep.

When the story is finished, Miss Martin says, "Your first day of school is over. Your mothers and fathers are outside."

Jake can't believe that his first whole day of school is over already. He has had such a good time.

He goes to his cubby hole to get his backpack. There he says good-bye to Judy.

"What a fun day!" he says.

"It was great!" says Judy.

After Jake puts on his backpack, he is sure to say good-bye to Miss Martin. She says, "See you tomorrow, Jake." Jake is happy that she remembers his name. He waves as he walks outside the classroom.

Jake's mother is waiting for him. Jake runs to her and says, "I have a surprise for you, Mom! I made it in school."

At home, Jake's mother tapes her wonderful surprise onto the refrigerator door. "I like this painting of a sun," she says.

"And I like school," says Jake.

Three Golden Flowers

Adapted by Lisa Harkrader
Illustrated by Marty Noble

There once was a chief who ruled an island tribe. The chief, his family, and his tribe lived happily on the island until one day the princess became sick. The chief called in the healers of the tribe. They gave the princess all the traditional remedies, but the princess became more ill. Finally, a tribal wise man came to see the chief.

"Find three golden orchids," the wise man said. "Their scent will cure the princess instantly. These flowers grow only where the sun shines through the water," said the wise man.

The chief was excited at this news! He would try anything.

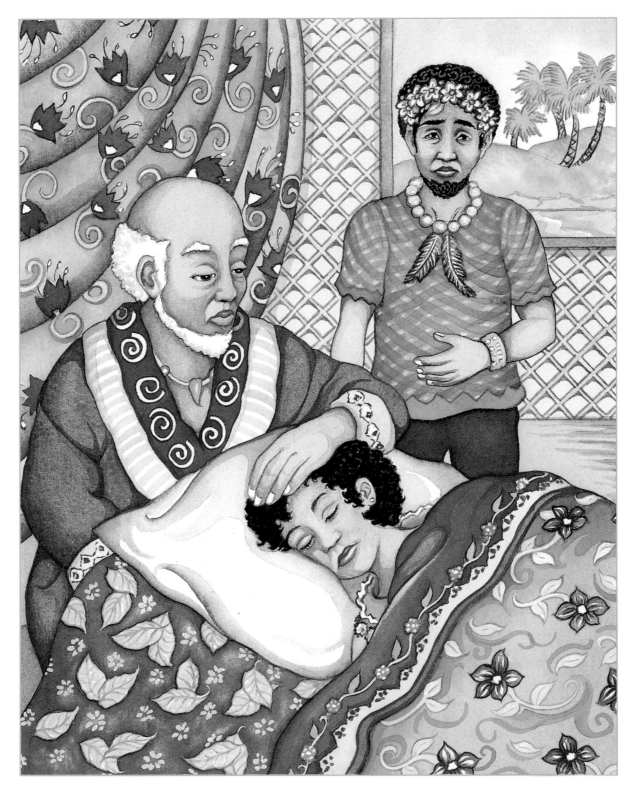

The chief issued a proclamation that any man who could bring three golden orchids and cure the princess could then marry her and inherit the kingdom.

When the great warriors of the kingdom heard the chief's proclamation, they explored every inch of the island, but they could not find the three golden orchids.

On a nearby island lived a poor man, his wife, and their three sons. The sons were not great warriors. They were farmers.

When the poor man and his family heard of the chief's proclamation, they became very excited. They had explored their island searching for fruits and herbs to feed themselves when their crops failed. They knew exactly where to find the flowers. Every year nine perfect orchids, delicate and golden, grew behind a waterfall in a hidden valley on the side of the mountain.

The oldest of the three brothers picked the three largest orchids. He placed them carefully in a basket and set off in his canoe across the sea.

When the oldest brother reached the island of the chief, he met an old fisherman on the beach.

"What have you there?" asked the fisherman.

The oldest brother knew that everyone was searching for the three golden orchids. He was afraid the old man would steal the basket if he knew what treasure lay inside.

"Worms," said the boy. "Fishing worms."

The fisherman smiled and let the boy continue on his way.

The oldest brother ran toward the chief's village. There he stood before the chief and opened his basket. But inside was nothing but worms, just as he had told the old fisherman.

The middle brother decided to try his luck. When he reached the island of the chief, he met the old fisherman. The fisherman asked the middle brother the same question as the older brother. The middle brother was also suspicious of the old man, and the same thing happened to his basket of flowers.

Now only three golden orchids remained. The youngest brother was determined to try. He picked the orchids and set off toward the island of the chief.

He met the old fisherman as soon as he reached the shore.

"What do you carry in your basket?" asked the fisherman.

The youngest boy was very honest. "I carry the flowers that will cure the princess."

"Indeed you do," said the old fisherman, as he gave the boy a bamboo flute. "This will bring you good luck. Use it wisely."

The youngest brother thanked the fisherman for the flute, then ran to the village with the orchids.

"I won't be tricked again," said the chief.

But the youngest brother opened his basket. Inside lay three golden orchids, as perfect as when he had first picked them.

The chief lifted them from the basket and arranged them on the princess's pillow.

The princess moved her head. Her eyes opened. She looked up and smiled.

"My daughter!" cried the chief. "You're cured."

She sat up to thank the youngest brother, and soon he and the princess were laughing and talking together.

"I'm so glad you were the one who brought the orchids," the princess told him. "You should have seen some of the rude and arrogant men who wanted to marry me."

But the chief was not as pleased. He was glad his daughter was healthy, but he had expected one of his great warriors to find the orchids. He did not want the princess to marry the son of a poor farmer. The chief thought of a plan.

"You've cured my daughter," he told the boy. "Now you must prove you are worthy to marry her. The princess keeps one hundred pet parrots. You must take them deep into the forest tomorrow morning. Then bring them back tomorrow night. If you do not return with all one hundred parrots, you will not marry my daughter."

The boy agreed, and the next morning he led the parrots into the forest. The birds flitted through the trees, this way and that. The boy spent the entire day chasing them, trying to keep them together. But by nightfall, he could not find one parrot.

He remembered the bamboo flute the fisherman had given him. He trilled a few notes. Like magic, all the parrots flew toward him from the trees. The boy set out through the forest, and the parrots followed.

He arrived at the chief's hut with all one hundred parrots.

The chief counted the birds. He counted them again. He called his advisors together, and they all counted the birds.

"One hundred parrots," said one advisor.

"I counted one hundred," said another.

"One hundred parrots exactly," they all agreed.

"He is worthy, Father," said the princess.

The chief stopped and looked at the boy. It was clear that the princess really liked this boy. The chief smiled. "You will make a fine husband for my daughter."

And so the poor farmer's son married the princess. He brought his parents and his brothers to the village to live amongst the tribe. The boy, the princess, their families, and their tribe all lived happily together in their kingdom.

The youngest son and the princess spent many days canoeing around the island. They loved watching the colorful parrots and enjoying each other's company.

Airport Adventure

Written by Sarah Toast
Illustrated by Steve Henry

Bump! Ginger's carrier rolls out of the jet's cargo bay. She can't wait to find her family after the long trip. Ginger pushes against the carrier door. It opens! Ginger bounds out of her carrier and runs straight past the man who refuels the airplane.

"Catch that dog!" he shouts.

Ginger does not know where she is going, but she is happy to be out of her carrier. She looks and looks for her family.

Suddenly she hears something. Maybe that is her family, she thinks. She runs toward the noise.

Ginger runs and runs. She runs into a room that is filled with suitcases.

"That's the hairiest suitcase I've ever seen," says someone.

"It's the fastest suitcase, too," says someone else.

Ginger runs in and out of the piles of suitcases. It is like a maze! One of these suitcases must belong to my family, thinks Ginger. She sniffs each suitcase as she runs by.

Ginger leaps onto a baggage cart. She sits on top of the many suitcases piled on the cart. When the cart stops suddenly, Ginger tumbles off.

"Whoa! Sorry, puppy," someone says to Ginger.

But Ginger is not hurt. She just wants to find her family. She knows that they must be close by.

Ginger jumps onto the moving conveyor belt that carries all baggage around the airport. Ginger thinks that the conveyor belt is scary and she does not like being bumped by the suitcases. But she is anxious to find her family. She looks all around, over and under each suitcase. On the conveyor belt, she rides through the small door with the suitcases.

The flaps covering the small doorway tickle Ginger's back as she rides through them on the suitcase mover.

"Woof!" Ginger is surprised to see a lot of people looking at her. They are waiting for their suitcases to come by. As Ginger rides around with the suitcases, she looks for her family in the crowd. Nobody looks familiar.

A boy notices Ginger. "Can I have that dog?" he asks. But before the little boy's mother can answer, Ginger jumps off of the conveyor belt.

Ginger wants to find her family. She does not see anybody she knows, but she smells something good! It's a little girl with an ice cream cone. Ginger realizes that she is hungry!

She runs over to the girl with the ice cream to see if she will share with her.

"Look, Mom! A puppy!" says the girl. "Can I give it some of my ice cream?"

"No, dear," says the girl's mother. "I'm sure that dog has a home and doesn't want your ice cream." The girl and her mother quickly leave the airport.

Ginger decides to leave the baggage claim area, too.

Soon Ginger comes to security. Here, people put their carry-on bags through x-ray machines so that guards can see what is inside. Then the passengers walk through metal detectors.

Metal detectors help the guards to be sure the passengers are not taking the wrong things on the airplanes.

When Ginger dashes through the metal detector, her dog tags set off the alarm. The alarm is very noisy!

People start running back and forth. They seem very serious.

"It was that dog!" she heard someone say.

"The dog set off the alarm!" says someone else.

Ginger runs fast to get away from the alarm. She comes to a room where people watch radar screens.

Ginger thinks that the radar screens look like TV sets. They remind her of being at home. My family likes to watch TV, thinks Ginger. Maybe they are around here.

The screens are actually for watching the planes. The air traffic controllers keep track of all the airplanes in the area. They speak to pilots by radio to help them fly and land their airplanes safely.

When one of the air traffic controllers gets up from his radar station to take a break, Ginger jumps onto his desk. Ginger can see most of the airport because the air traffic controllers work in the tall airport tower. She watches as an airplane taxis down the runway, then speeds up and takes off.

She thinks the airplanes look like giant birds. Back at home, she watches birds in the backyard all the time. These birds are very noisy, though, thinks Ginger.

Ginger watches another airplane come in for a landing. Then she sees a man near the airport terminal waving orange sticks. The way the man waves the sticks tells the pilot how to drive the airplane and where to park it. But Ginger knows all about sticks. She thinks the man is playing her favorite game.

Ginger gets very excited as she watches the man wave the sticks back and forth. Okay, I'm ready to play, thinks Ginger.

She jumps down off of the controller's desk to find the man with the sticks. I bet I will get a treat if I bring the sticks back to him, too, thinks Ginger.

Ginger nearly knocks down two controllers on her way out.

Ginger can't wait to play the stick game. She runs out of the tower control room. When she sees an open elevator door, Ginger scoots in the elevator. It isn't long before the door closes and Ginger rides down.

When the door opens again, Ginger smells fresh air. She runs down a hallway and out an open door. Ginger dashes outside to find the man with the orange sticks.

There he is! Ginger races up to him and snatches one of the orange sticks.

"Catch that dog!" shouts another worker, who drops his wrench and chases after Ginger.

Ginger thinks that this is all part of the game. She starts to run faster. Boy, this is the most fun she's had since arriving at the airport! Ginger runs and runs.

All the trucks and workers on the runways stop what they are doing. They all look at Ginger.

"Somebody stop that dog!" a man yells.

But nobody can catch up with her. Ginger likes this game, but she is beginning to get tired.

Ginger runs with the stick into a huge building where many people are working on a big jet airplane. People are using lots of noisy tools to repair the airplane and make sure it is ready to fly. But Ginger doesn't waste time exploring. She smells food!

A nice mechanic holds out half of his sandwich to Ginger. When Ginger drops the orange stick to gobble the sandwich, the nice mechanic pats her on the head. Ginger licks his hand. She knew she would get a treat!

"Where did you come from?" the mechanic asks.

Ginger just wags her tail. She would really like it here if it weren't so noisy.

Ginger finishes the sandwich and inspects the mechanic's lunchbox for more treats.

The mechanic laughs. "Boy, you are really hungry, huh? I bet you are thirsty, too." The mechanic pours some water from his thermos into a small dish.

Ginger drinks noisily.

"I think you got more water on the floor than in your tummy," laughs the mechanic.

When Ginger is finished drinking, the nice mechanic takes her to the place where traveling animals wait for their families.

"Don't worry," says the mechanic, "I know where you belong."

When Ginger spots her carrier, she runs away from the mechanic.

"Catch that dog!" shouts a worker. But Ginger speeds past him, hurries inside her carrier, then settles down for a nap.

It is nice to be in the quiet carrier, thinks Ginger as she drifts off to sleep.

When Ginger's family comes to get her, she is still fast asleep.

"Look at our sleepyhead!" Father says.

"Wake up, Ginger," says Mother. "You must be ready to get out and stretch your legs."

"You should see the airport," says the little boy. "There are so many neat things here. I bet you are tired of being cooped up in that little carrier."

Ginger just yawns and gives the boy a hello lick.

Henny Penny

Adapted by Carolyn Quattrocki
Illustrated by Tim Ellis

One fine day Henny Penny was eating corn in the small yard beside her house. The sun was shining. There was not a cloud in the sky. And Henny Penny stood under a large oak tree.

Suddenly, boink! An acorn fell out of the tree and hit Henny Penny right on the top of her head. Henny Penny did not know what to think at first—she was a little dazed. Then she knew exactly what happened!

"Oh, my!" she cried. "The sky is falling! The sky is falling! I must go and tell the king."

Of course if the sky were falling, the king would want to know. So Henny Penny tied a scarf around her head, in case more pieces of sky started to fall, and she gathered up a basketful of corn to eat on her journey. Then she set off down the road to tell the king that the sky was falling.

On her way she passed the house of Cocky Locky. Cocky Locky was working hard, building a new porch. He obviously had not heard the news about the sky falling.

"Henny Penny, where are you going?" he called.

"Oh, Cocky Locky, the sky is falling, and I am going to tell the king!" said Henny Penny.

"How do you know it is falling?" asked Cocky Locky.

"I saw it with my own eyes and heard it with my own ears, and a piece of it fell on my head!" said Henny Penny.

"Then I will go with you to tell the king," Cocky Locky said to Henny Penny. The two set off down the road to tell the king. They knew they must hurry.

What good is a new porch if the sky is falling, anyway? thought Cocky Locky.

Henny Penny and Cocky Locky went along until they met Ducky Lucky. Ducky Lucky was just returning from her morning swim; she must not have heard the news either.

"Good morning, Henny Penny and Cocky Locky," said Ducky Lucky. "Where are you going?"

"The sky is falling, and we are going to tell the king," said Cocky Locky.

"How do you know the sky is falling?" asked Ducky Lucky.

"Henny Penny told me," said Cocky Locky.

"I saw it with my own eyes and heard it with my own ears, and a piece of it fell on my head!" said Henny Penny.

"Oh, my! That is serious. Then I will go with both of you to tell the king," said Ducky Lucky. And she did.

So Henny Penny, Cocky Locky, and Ducky Lucky all set off to tell the king.

All three of them kept looking up as they walked to make sure that more sky did not fall on their heads. Because they were all looking up, they began to bump into each other as they walked.

"Maybe we should watch for the sky in shifts," they decided.

Henny Penny, Cocky Locky, and Ducky Lucky went along until they met Goosey Loosey. Goosey Loosey was busy selling vegetables at her roadside stand. She obviously hadn't heard the terrible news yet.

"Good morning, Henny Penny, Cocky Locky, and Ducky Lucky," said Goosey Loosey. "Where are you going?"

"The sky is falling, and we are going to tell the king," said Ducky Lucky.

"How do you know it is falling?" asked Goosey Loosey.

"Cocky Locky told me," said Ducky Lucky.

"Henny Penny told me," said Cocky Locky.

"I saw it with my own eyes and heard it with my own ears, and a piece of it fell on my head!" said Henny Penny, pointing to the lump on her head where the sky hit her.

"That's very bad news. It won't be good for vegetable sales, either. Then I must go with you to tell the king," said Goosey Loosey bravely.

So Henny Penny, Cocky Locky, Ducky Lucky, and Goosey Loosey all set off to tell the king together.

Henny Penny, Cocky Locky, Ducky Lucky, and Goosey Loosey all went along until they met Turkey Lurkey out in front of his garden. He was pretty calm, so Henny Penny knew that Turkey Lurkey did not know the bad news yet.

"Good morning, Henny Penny, Cocky Locky, Ducky Lucky, and Goosey Loosey," said Turkey Lurkey. "Where are all of you going on this fine day?"

"The sky is falling and we are going to tell the king," said Goosey Loosey.

"How do you know it is falling?" asked Turkey Lurkey.

"Ducky Lucky told me," said Goosey Loosey.

"Cocky Locky told me," said Ducky Lucky.

"Henny Penny told me," said Cocky Locky.

"I saw it with my own eyes and heard it with my own ears, and a piece of it fell on my head!" said Henny Penny.

"You don't say! Well, then I'll go with you to tell the king," said Turkey Lurkey.

So Henny Penny, Cocky Locky, Ducky Lucky, Goosey Loosey, and Turkey Lurkey all set off to tell the king together.

They all went along until they met up with Foxy Loxy. Now Foxy Loxy always seems to have the latest news, but he did not seem worried about the sky.

"Good morning," said Foxy Loxy. "Where are you going?"

"The sky is falling, and we are going to tell the king," said Turkey Lurkey.

"How do you know it is falling?" asked Foxy Loxy.

"Goosey Loosey told me," said Turkey Lurkey.

"Ducky Lucky told me," said Goosey Loosey.

"Cocky Locky told me," said Ducky Lucky.

"Henny Penny told me," said Cocky Locky.

"I saw it with my own eyes and heard it with my own ears, and a piece of it fell on my head!" said Henny Penny.

"Oh, yes! I thought I read about that in today's news. Yes, well then you should come with me. I will show you a shorter way to the king's palace," said Foxy Loxy.

So Henny Penny, Cocky Locky, Ducky Lucky, Goosey Loosey, and Turkey Lurkey said to Foxy Loxy, "Oh, yes, please show us the shorter way to the king's palace."

"Yes," said Henny Penny, "we would be very grateful to you because we must hurry to tell him that the sky is falling."

"Just follow me, Henny Penny, Cocky Locky, Ducky Lucky, Goosey Loosey, and Turkey Lurkey," said Foxy Loxy. "We'll go right up this hill and across this bridge and down this road. Before you know it, we'll be at the king's palace. And you can all tell him that the sky is falling!"

Henny Penny, Cocky Locky, Ducky Lucky, Goosey Loosey, and Turkey Lurkey all followed Foxy Loxy.

Soon they came to the entrance of a dark cave. What Henny Penny, Cocky Locky, Ducky Lucky, Goosey Loosey, and Turkey Lurkey did not know was that this cave was really Foxy Loxy's home! Foxy Loxy was trying to trick them all.

"Just follow me through here," said Foxy Loxy, "and we'll soon be at the king's palace."

Cocky Locky, Ducky Lucky, Goosey Loosey, and Turkey Lurkey all followed Foxy Loxy into the cave. Henny Penny was last in line, and she was frightened. She felt that something was not right. She started to run away.

Henny Penny ran and ran as fast as her legs would carry her. She ran back along the winding road. She ran across the narrow bridge. And she ran down the steep hill.

Henny Penny quickly ran past Turkey Lurkey's garden. She ran past the place where Goosey Loosey had set up her roadside stand. She ran past Ducky Lucky's pond, and Henny Penny ran past Cocky Locky's house.

Henny Penny ran and ran until, up ahead, she saw her cozy little house with the oak tree beside it. She could even see the corn scattered on the ground underneath the tree.

Henny Penny ran all the way to her front porch! She was last seen scratching happily for corn in her little yard. And the king never did hear that the sky was falling.

Henny Penny heard that Cocky Locky, Ducky Lucky, Goosey Loosey, and Turkey Lurkey started running right after her, but she was so scared that she didn't look back. And Henny Penny was so embarrassed about thinking that the sky was falling that she never saw her friends again.

Ziggy's Fine Coat

Written by Megan Musgrave
Illustrated by Debbie Pinkney

Ziggy was a handsome young tiger cub who lived in the jungle with his parents. His mother was the most kind tigress in all of the jungle, and his father was the most mighty tiger. But Ziggy never felt like he fit in. His stripes always made him feel out of place.

One day Ziggy and his father went to the watering hole for a drink. He looked at his reflection in the shiny surface of the water. All he saw were stripes, stripes, and more stripes.

"Dad, just look at all these stripes," said Ziggy sadly. "Your stripes and Mama's seem to fit you, but mine are funny-looking."

"Son, you have brighter and bolder zigzag stripes than any other cub in the jungle," said his father. "That's why we named you Ziggy. Don't worry. You'll grow into your stripes one day."

That didn't make Ziggy feel much better. He thought and thought as he wandered through his jungle home.

"There must be some way to get rid of these stripes," Ziggy muttered to himself.

Just then, Ziggy's parrot friend Kiko swooped down and landed in a big flower bush. Kiko meant to land *on* the bush, but he wasn't good at landings. "What's the matter, Ziggy?" asked Kiko.

"I don't want to be striped anymore," Ziggy explained.

Kiko hopped out of the big flower bush. "Maybe these bright red flowers could help," suggested Kiko.

Ziggy stared at the beautiful flowers. Suddenly, he came up with an idea.

"Those flower petals just might do the trick!" he said.

Ziggy carefully plucked some of the flower petals from the bush. Then he licked his coat and pasted the petals all over himself. Soon, all of his black stripes were covered.

"Not a stripe in sight!" said Kiko gleefully.

No sooner had Kiko said this, though, then a strong breeze blew through the jungle. The breeze blew all of Ziggy's beautiful flower petals away.

"Oh, no," cried Ziggy. "My big old stripes are back again."

Just then, Ziggy's monkey friend Maka swung down from a nearby tree. "Why the long face?" asked Maka.

"I'm tired of always being striped. I wish I could find a way to get rid of these silly stripes once and for all," sighed Ziggy.

Maka thought only for a short while. The mischievous monkey was always full of good ideas.

"I have just the thing for you," laughed Maka. "Why don't you paint your stripes with mud?"

Ziggy and Maka ran over to a big mud puddle near the local watering hole. "This is just the thing!" said Ziggy.

Ziggy pounced right into the middle of the puddle. Then he rolled around in the soft, squishy mud.

"Be sure to get good and muddy!" Maka shouted. "We want to cover up each and every one of those pesky stripes!"

Ziggy squirmed and wiggled around in the mud. Before long, every last one of his stripes was covered in the thick, brown mud.

Just then, Ziggy's mother came to the watering hole and saw Ziggy rolling in the mud. She nudged him over to the water and scrubbed all the mud off of his coat.

"But, Mama," Ziggy complained, "I don't want to be striped anymore. Don't you ever get tired of being striped?"

"When I was your age, I didn't want to be striped, either," his mother said. "But then I learned that my coat is very special. And your coat is special, too."

"I guess so," sighed Ziggy, as he hung his head.

Then Ziggy's mother had an idea. "Let's play a game," she said as they walked toward the jungle. "Close your eyes and count to ten, and then try to find me."

"All right, Mother," sighed Ziggy.

Ziggy had played hide-and-seek before, and he didn't see what it had to do with his stripes. But Ziggy counted anyway.

When Ziggy got to ten, he opened his eyes and looked around. "Ready or not, here I come!" he yelled.

Ziggy looked around for his mother. He looked in the tall grasses. He looked behind a tree and a bush. He checked over by the watering hole and in the mud puddle. He looked in the flower bush and behind a termite mound. But she was nowhere to be found.

"Mother, where are you?" called Ziggy.

"Why, I'm right here, Ziggy," said his mother, stepping out from the tall grasses right in front of him.

"But I didn't see you there at all!" exclaimed Ziggy.

"That's why our stripes are so special. Our orange stripes blend in with the grasses, and our black stripes blend in with the dark shadows. They make it easy for us to hide," his mother smiled.

"I guess these old stripes are not so bad after all!" giggled Ziggy. "I'm going to play with Kiko and Maka." He could hardly wait to show his friends his new trick.

The Gingerbread Man

Adapted by Priscilla I. Langhorn
Illustrated by Tricia Zimic

One morning, before he went to work in his garden, an old man said to his wife, "Will you bake me some gingerbread to go with my tea today?"

The old woman decided to make a gingerbread man. She gave him two candy eyes, three candy buttons, and a sweet smile. Then she popped the gingerbread man into the oven to bake.

When the woman opened the oven, the gingerbread man jumped out and quickly ran away!

"Run, run as fast as you can! You can't catch me, I'm the gingerbread man!" said the gingerbread man.

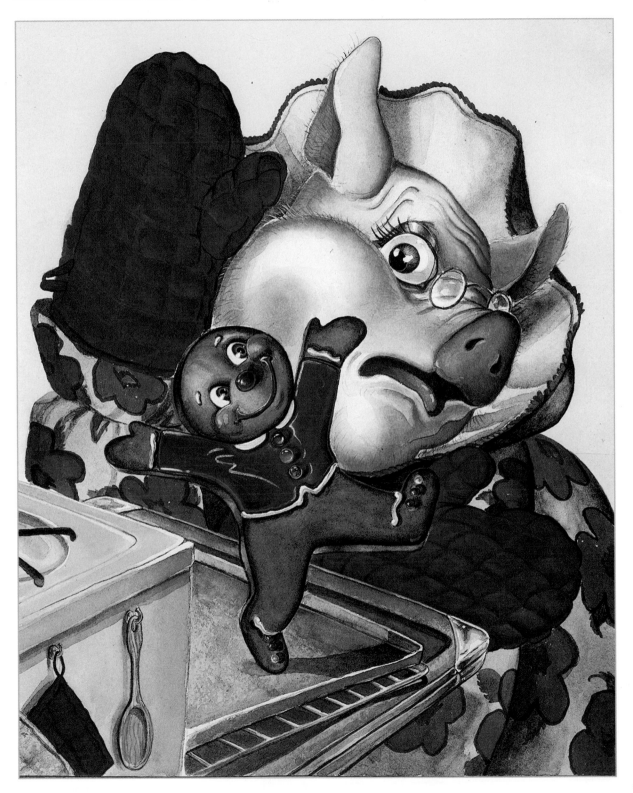

The old woman ran after the gingerbread man, but she could not catch him.

The gingerbread man ran through the garden, right past the old man working in the field.

"Stop, gingerbread man, stop! You are my teatime treat!" called the old man. But the gingerbread man did not stop.

"Run, run as fast as you can! You can't catch me, I'm the gingerbread man!" laughed the gingerbread man.

The surprised old woman and grumpy old man chased after the gingerbread man, but the little cookie ran faster. He looked over his shoulder and laughed.

"Run, run as fast as you can! You can't catch me, I'm the gingerbread man!" said the gingerbread man. He ran and ran.

He ran past a tomcat fishing in the pond.

"Stop, gingerbread man, stop! You look good enough to eat!" meowed the tomcat. But the gingerbread man just ran faster than ever. He just looked at the tomcat and smiled.

"Run, run as fast as you can! You can't catch me, I'm the gingerbread man!" called the gingerbread man.

The old woman, old man, and tomcat chased the gingerbread man through the field. But he ran much too fast for them to catch him.

The gingerbread man ran past a young calf.

"Stop, gingerbread man, stop! I want to get a taste of you!" mooed the calf. But the frisky gingerbread man ran faster!

"Run, run as fast as you can! You can't catch me, I'm the gingerbread man!" said the gingerbread man.

The old woman, old man, tomcat, and young calf chased after the gingerbread man. But he ran on and on and on.

"Run, run as fast as you can! You can't catch me, I'm the gingerbread man!" said the gingerbread man.

Next he ran past a pretty, little white pony picking apples. She saw the little cookie running by.

"Stop, gingerbread man, stop! I'd like to nibble those sweet candy buttons of yours!" said the pony. The gingerbread man kept right on running.

"Run, run as fast as you can! You can't catch me, I'm the gingerbread man!" yelled the gingerbread man.

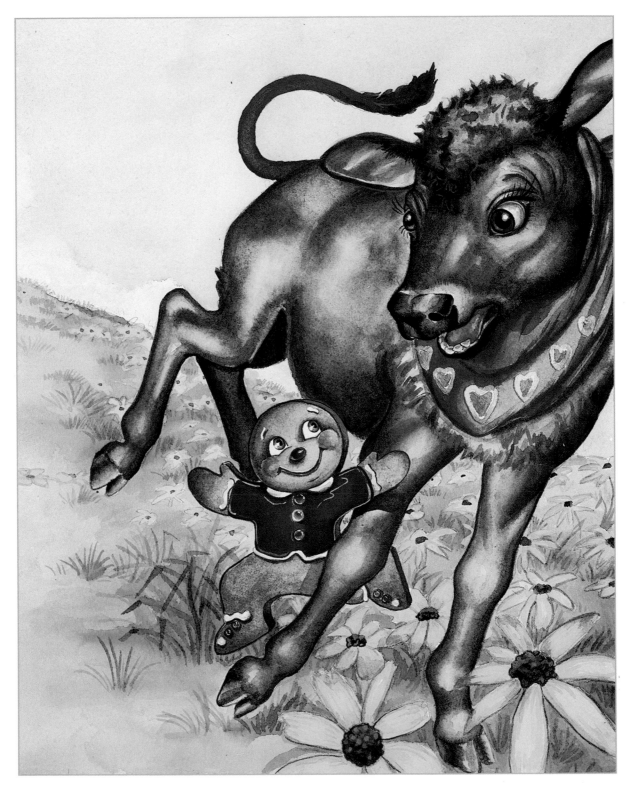

The old woman, old man, tomcat, young calf, and pretty little pony ran after the gingerbread man.

"Run, run as fast as you can! You can't catch me, I'm the gingerbread man!" said the gingerbread man.

The gingerbread man ran past a big farm dog who was digging for bones.

"Stop, gingerbread man, stop! You'd make a fine dessert with my dinner!" barked the farm dog. The gingerbread man did not even slow down.

He said as he ran by, "Run, run as fast as you can! You can't catch me, I'm the gingerbread man!"

The old woman, old man, tomcat, young calf, pretty little pony, and big farm dog chased the gingerbread man.

"Run, run as fast as you can! You can't catch me, I'm the gingerbread man!" the gingerbread man laughed.

The gingerbread man ran past a mama duck gathering berries for her family.

"Stop, gingerbread man, stop! My ducklings would like you for a snack!" quacked the duck. The gingerbread man just laughed.

"Run, run as fast as you can! You can't catch me, I'm the gingerbread man!" cried the gingerbread man.

The old woman, old man, tomcat, young calf, pretty little pony, big farm dog, and mama duck chased the gingerbread man. But the gingerbread man ran faster and faster.

The gingerbread man ran past a busy beaver chopping down a tall fir tree.

"Stop, gingerbread man, stop! I want to eat you right now!" said the beaver. The gingerbread man did not slow down. He just laughed a silly laugh.

"Run, run as fast as you can! You can't catch me, I'm the gingerbread man!" said the gingerbread man.

The old woman, old man, tomcat, young calf, pretty little pony, big farm dog, mama duck, and busy beaver were far behind the gingerbread man.

They could not catch him!

Next the little gingerbread man ran past a rabbit munching on some vegetables.

"I know I'm faster than you," said the rabbit.

But as fast as the bunny ran, the rabbit could not catch up to the little gingerbread man, either. He joined the old woman, old man, tomcat, young calf, pretty little pony, big farm dog, mama duck, and busy beaver in the chase.

Then it looked like they might catch the gingerbread man after all. The cookie couldn't get across water without melting.

So, the gingerbread man was stopped at the bank of a wide stream. On the bank, a fox was sunning himself.

"I'll help you cross this river, gingerbread man. Just hop on my back, and I'll give you a ride," said the fox.

The gingerbread man was not sure that this was a good idea, but he had a big, hungry group chasing him. He felt as though he had no choice.

The gingerbread man quickly hopped on the fox's back. "Take me to the other side!" yelled the gingerbread man.

As the gingerbread man floated off on the fox's back, he looked at the old woman, old man, tomcat, young calf, pretty little pony, big farm dog, mama duck, busy beaver, and bunny rabbit all jumping up and down on the shore.

The gingerbread man just laughed at the sight of them and shouted, "Run, run as fast as you can! You can't catch me, I'm the gingerbread man!"

The fox turned to the gingerbread man and said, "Watch out or you will get wet, gingerbread man. Climb onto my head where you will be safe and dry."

The gingerbread man was so excited to have left the hungry group on the shore, that he did not realize that this was a bad idea. He thought he was safe.

The gingerbread man hopped right onto the fox's head.

Then the fox said, "My, it is getting quite deep! You better climb onto my nose to stay dry."

The gingerbread man listened to the fox. He wanted to make sure he stayed dry.

Just then, the fox opened his mouth wide and gobbled up the gingerbread man.

And that was the end of the gingerbread man!

Guess What They're Building

Written by Sarah Toast
Illustrated by Steve Henry

Jenny and Josh are walking home from school a new way when they see a tall fence with big holes cut in it like round windows. They look through the holes and see an old, empty building with all of its doors and windows boarded up.

"I wonder why there is a fence around this old building," says Josh. He peeks farther into the hole.

"I bet they're going to tear it down soon and build something else here," says Jenny. "Let's come back tomorrow to see what's happening."

The next day when Jenny and Josh look through the holes in the fence, they see a huge crane. The operator of the crane swings a big wrecking ball on a long chain. The large ball smashes against the old building. Bricks and glass shatter. The ball crashes into the old building again and again.

"Tearing down a building sure is noisy and messy," says Jenny.

"Isn't it cool?" says Josh.

"That ball must be very heavy," says Jenny.

"Yeah. I bet it's really a monster's bowling ball!" says Josh. "I bet this is how monsters bowl."

"Well, that makes sense, since monsters wouldn't fit in regular bowling alleys," says Jenny. "But I don't see any monsters around here, do you?"

Josh looks around. "Well, I guess not. Maybe the monster just loaned the construction worker his bowling ball for the day."

Jenny laughs. "That's an awfully nice monster!"

Josh and Jenny laugh together as they watch more and more of the building come down.

As they walk home, they keep their eye out for monsters.

The following week when Jenny and Josh look through the fence, they see a bulldozer digging and scraping dirt into piles.

A power shovel scoops up dirt and loads it into a big dump truck. The dump truck hauls the dirt away.

Jenny says, "Those scooping and digging machines must be trying to dig a tunnel all the way to China!"

The next time Jenny and Josh look at the tunnel to China, they see that it isn't very deep. Instead, the hole is getting a cement bottom and cement sides.

A steamroller smooths out the bottom. Then workers spread the wet cement before it hardens.

Josh says, "They must be building the world's largest swimming pool ever!"

"Maybe it's a present for the monster for letting them use his bowling ball," says Jenny.

"I don't think monsters like to go swimming, though," says Josh. "But maybe it is a sea monster!"

Jenny and Josh think about a giant sea monster swimming in the world's biggest swimming pool.

When Jenny and Josh go back many days later to see if the world's largest swimming pool is full of water yet, they are pretty surprised.

What they see instead of a swimming pool is a huge frame being built. Three cranes lift heavy steel beams into place.

"This isn't the world's largest swimming pool," says Jenny. "Maybe it's a jungle gym for a giant!"

"I hope it is a friendly giant that will let us play on the jungle gym, too," says Josh.

Jenny and Josh imagine the giant who likes to play. It seems that only a good-natured giant would want a giant jungle gym. They agree that this giant must be friendly.

They can't wait until the jungle gym is finished so that they can meet the giant and be his friend.

"It would be very useful to have a giant as a friend," says Josh.

"Yes, we would always have the best seats at a ball game. We could just sit on the giant's shoulders!" says Jenny.

They both laugh and agree to visit the jungle gym in a few days to see if it is finished.

A few days later when Jenny and Josh go to the giant jungle gym, a worker invites them to look around. They can't wait to see what it looks like.

"Take a peek down there," says the worker.

They look inside a room and see hollow arms reaching in all directions. Wires and pipes go in and out of the arms.

"Yikes! I think we've found a robot octopus!" says Josh.

"The jungle gym must really be a cage to keep the giant octopus in," says Jenny.

"We were right," says Josh. "It is a sea monster!"

Jenny and Josh look around a little more. Then the worker tells them that their break time is over, and Jenny and Josh must leave.

"It gets too dangerous for little kids when we're working. We wouldn't want you two to get hurt," says the worker.

"Thank you for letting us look," say Jenny and Josh.

As Jenny and Josh head for home, they begin to think about what the worker said.

"I bet the worker was worried that the octopus would hurt us," said Josh. "It's a good thing we left when we did."

It is a long time before Jenny and Josh return to see the robot octopus. When they finally return and look through the fence, they see workers standing on hanging platforms to lay bricks.

Jenny and Josh watch for a long time. Laying bricks is slow work because each brick has to be placed just right.

"This is some kind of new building, not a giant jungle gym with a robot octopus living inside," says Josh.

"Who do you think will live here? A king and queen?" asks Jenny. "I hope they're nice."

"Look at the doorway," says Josh. "It's a great big dog house for a giant's great big dog!"

"Oh, won't that be fun!" says Jenny. "I just love dogs!"

"This dog will want to fetch whole trees, not just sticks," laughs Josh.

Jenny and Josh watch the workers place more bricks. They talk about the giant dog and how fun it will be to watch it run and play. They can't wait to see what kind of dog a giant would have.

"A Great Dane, maybe?" says Josh.

"Or perhaps a St. Bernard," says Jenny.

Jenny and Josh go back soon to see what kind of dog the giant has. They hope it is friendly. What they see instead is a crane placing large stone columns all across the front of the giant dog house. They are surprised.

"This is not a big house for a giant dog," says Josh. He looks very sad.

"Cheer up, Josh," says Jenny. "This must be a really strong, really huge cage! A dinosaur lives in there!"

"Yeah! Maybe even lots of dinosaurs!" grins Josh.

Jenny and Josh go to the dinosaur cage every day to catch sight of the dinosaurs living there. The only thing they see is that the fence with the peepholes has been taken down.

But one day they get a big surprise. They can hardly believe their eyes when a huge dinosaur skeleton is rolled between two cage bars and right into the big building.

"Wow!" says Jenny. "We guessed right this time! It is a dinosaur cage after all!"

"It doesn't look like this dinosaur is going to escape, though," says Josh.

Finally, the building is finished! It is a dinosaur museum. Jenny and Josh are so excited that they are the first in line.

"It's too bad that there are no monsters or giant dogs living here," says Josh.

"Yeah, but if giants or monsters lived here, we might not be able to visit after school," says Jenny. "They might not be the kind of monsters that are friendly."

"I bet you are right," says Josh. "It would depend a lot on the monsters' moods. We couldn't come over if they were cranky."

Jenny and Josh decide that it is better that a sea monster or a giant or a robot octopus doesn't live in the museum. They like to visit the new building on their way home from school.

Jenny and Josh love to look at the fossils and statues at the dinosaur museum. But they think one of the best things about the museum is that they saw how it was built.

The Flying Prince

Adapted by Brian Conway
Illustrated by Kathi Ember

Prince Rashar lived in a distant land. He spent each day hunting and exploring the jungle. One day while hunting, a large parrot landed beside Prince Rashar.

"I am the king of the parrots," it said proudly. "This is our kingdom, and you are not welcome here."

"I will not harm you," promised Prince Rashar. "How is it that you can talk?"

"Princess Saledra gave me that power, so I can protect my subjects from hunters," answered the Parrot King. "She is our guardian. She is the kindest and most beautiful princess!"

"Where can I find her?" Prince Rashar asked the parrot.

"You could never reach her," squawked the Parrot King. "She lives many kingdoms away, in the city where night becomes day."

Prince Rashar thought of nothing but the princess for many days. He decided that he must find the beautiful Princess Saledra. He strapped his bow and arrow to his back and rode off.

The prince traveled for four days. Suddenly, Prince Rashar heard shouting. He saw four trolls having a terrible argument.

"Excuse me," the prince said calmly. "Perhaps I can help you."

"Our master left us these four magic things," the trolls answered. "But he did not tell us who gets what!"

There was a flying bed that would take its owner wherever he wished to go. There was a cloth bag that would give its holder anything he wished for. There was a bowl that filled with water upon command, and a stick tied to a rope, which could defeat and tie up even the strongest foes.

"I can help you decide fairly," said the clever prince. "I will shoot an arrow into the jungle. Whoever returns with the arrow shall keep all the magic items."

The trolls agreed to the plan. So Prince Rashar shot an arrow into the air, and the trolls dashed into the jungle to find it.

While the trolls searched for the arrow, Prince Rashar took the magic items. He rolled out the bed and sat down on it.

"Magic bed, take me to the city where night becomes day," he commanded. "Take me to the city where Princess Saledra lives!"

The magic bed lifted the prince high above the jungle, then it zoomed through the air. At last the bed settled down at the gates of a distant city. Prince Rashar stopped an old woman.

"I've come to see Princess Saledra," he told her.

"Nobody sees the princess until nightfall," said the woman.

The prince was disappointed. He did not want to wait.

"Go to the palace and wait for darkness," said the old woman.

The prince hurried to the palace. When the sun set, the city was dark for a moment. Then a door opened at the roof of the palace. Princess Saledra walked out from her room and stepped across the palace rooftop.

Her beauty shone more brightly than the moon. In an instant, night became day, and the princess was the reason.

Prince Rashar could not take his eyes off her. At that moment, he knew he must meet the beautiful princess.

Prince Rashar took his bag of wishes and said, "Bag, give me a silk shawl, one that matches the princess's gown exactly."

He reached into the bag to find a flowing silk shawl.

"Magic bed, take me to the room at the top of the palace, where Princess Saledra sleeps," he said.

The magic bed lifted the prince over the city. It landed on the palace roof, and the prince crept through the door to the princess's room.

Though the room was as bright as day, with not a lamp in sight, Princess Saledra was sleeping soundly in her bed. The prince quietly set the shawl beside her bed. He stopped to gaze upon her beautiful face before he left. He had never seen anyone more beautiful. He knew he loved her.

The next morning, the princess awoke to find the beautiful shawl, as fine as the gown she wore. But her gown was one of a kind, spun with special silk. Princess Saledra was very curious about who her secret admirer might be.

"He must be a man of great courage," she guessed, "to sneak into my father's palace at night. And to make such a perfect shawl, he must have magic as strong as my own!"

That night, after the princess had fallen asleep, Prince Rashar ordered a very special gift for the princess.

"Bag," he said, "give me a diamond ring for Princess Saledra."

A ring appeared in the bag that matched the princess's jewels. The magic bed carried the prince to the princess's room. But this time she awoke with a start. At first, she was frightened.

"Who are you?" she demanded.

"I am Prince Rashar," answered the prince. "I have come from a distant country, just to meet you."

The princess looked at the prince. He was very handsome, and he spoke from his heart. Her heart softened further when she looked at his gift. The ring matched her own jewels perfectly.

The princess smiled the brightest smile ever seen.

Prince Rashar and Princess Saledra fell in love instantly. They were married the next day. Then Prince Rashar and Princess Saledra flew over their kingdom on the magic bed.

Three Billy Goats Gruff

Adapted by Carolyn Quattrocki
Illustrated by Tim Ellis

Once there were three Billy Goats Gruff. The oldest was Big Billy Goat Gruff who wore a collar of thick black leather. Middle Billy Goat Gruff had a red collar around his neck, and Little Billy Goat Gruff wore a yellow one.

Big Billy Goat Gruff had a deep, gruff billy goat voice. Middle Billy Goat Gruff had a middle-sized billy goat voice. And Little Billy Goat Gruff had a very high, little billy goat voice.

All winter long, the three Billy Goats Gruff lived on a rocky hillside. They loved to run and jump. Right next to their hill ran a powerful, rushing river.

Every day during the cold winter months, the three Billy Goats Gruff played among the rocks.

Little Billy Goat Gruff would cry in his little billy goat voice, "Watch this!" as he leaped over little rocks.

Middle Billy Goat Gruff would call, "Watch this!" as he leaped over middle-sized rocks.

Big Billy Goat Gruff would say in his big billy goat voice, "WATCH THIS!" as he leaped over great big rocks.

Big Billy Goat Gruff was the best climber and the strongest of the three billy goats. He had strong legs and big, curved horns. Big Billy Goat Gruff was also the smartest of the three billy goats. Whenever there was a problem, Big Billy Goat Gruff was the one to find a solution.

Middle Billy Goat Gruff and Little Billy Goat Gruff would have fun watching Big Billy Goat Gruff jump over the biggest rocks and the steepest ravines. They liked to challenge the big goat to see what he could do. Big Billy Goat Gruff liked the challenges because they made him feel bigger and mightier than even the mountain range.

At night the wind would blow coldly over the three Billy Goats Gruff. Little Billy Goat Gruff looked up to see a sky filled with bright, shining stars.

Middle Billy Goat Gruff looked up at the night to see the thin sliver of a winter moon.

Big Billy Goat Gruff said, "Enough looking at the sky, it is time to find a place to sleep."

So the three Billy Goats Gruff found a nice, cozy cave to sleep in for the night.

"Good night," said Big Billy Goat Gruff in his big billy goat voice. He tucked in the other goats.

"Good night," said Middle Billy Goat Gruff in his middle-sized billy goat voice.

"Good night," said Little Billy Goat Gruff in his little billy goat voice. Then they would all lay down together on those cold winter nights and dream of springtime.

Sometimes, when Little Billy Goat Gruff could not sleep, Big Billy Goat Gruff made shadows on the cave wall. Not only was Big Billy Goat Gruff big and tough, but he had a big heart, too.

Soon it was springtime. From their rocky hillside the three Billy Goats Gruff looked longingly across the rushing river.

"How I would love to go up the mountain across the river," said Little Billy Goat Gruff. "The grass is green, and the flowers are pretty. There is plenty to eat on that side."

"To get to the mountain," said Middle Billy Goat Gruff, "we will have to cross the bridge over the river."

The three Billy Goats Gruff knew that under the bridge lived a mean, ugly troll. The troll had eyes that were as big as saucers, a head of shaggy hair, and a nose that was as long as a broomstick.

The evil troll always said that he would eat any billy goats that tried to cross the bridge. He was a nasty troll indeed.

"You two cannot go across the bridge," said Big Billy Goat Gruff. "It is not safe." He was always looking out for the other two billy goats.

So the three Billy Goats Gruff stayed on their rocky side of the river and played and jumped. They had many animal friends on their side of the river that were also too afraid to cross the bridge. Still, they wanted to see what was on the other side.

Every day the Billy Goats Gruff looked across the river. Just once they would like to visit.

"The grass looks so sweet over there," said Little Billy Goat Gruff. "Let's go over the bridge."

"The flowers smell like honey!" said Middle Billy Goat Gruff. "Yes, let's go over the bridge."

"But what are we to do about the troll?" asked Big Billy Goat Gruff. They all shook their heads sadly.

They decided to play hide-and-seek amongst the rocks on their side of the river instead. Big Billy Goat Gruff was always "It" because it was hard for him to find a hiding spot big enough. Little Billy Goat Gruff always won.

One day, as they were looking at the green mountain, Big Billy Goat Gruff had an idea. He thought of a plan to trick the troll so that they could cross the bridge to the other side. Maybe Big Billy Goat Gruff was tired of always being "It" when they played hide-and-seek, and maybe that is what sparked his plan to get across the bridge.

Anyway, the three billy goats were excited to hear the plan!

The three billy goats got together and talked about Big Billy Goat Gruff's plan to get to the other side. They talked and talked. Big Billy Goat Gruff even drew pictures to help Little Billy Goat Gruff understand. Then the plan was set.

The next morning the three Billy Goats Gruff went down to the river. Little Billy Goat Gruff started to cross the bridge.

Trip-trap, trip-trap, trip-trap, went Little Billy Goat Gruff's feet on the bridge.

"Who's that trip-trapping across my bridge?" roared the troll.

"It is only I, Little Billy Goat Gruff," said Little Billy Goat Gruff quietly.

"I'm coming to eat you up!" said the troll.

"Oh, no!" said Little Billy Goat Gruff. "I am only a tiny, little billy goat. Wait for my brother, Middle Billy Goat Gruff. He will make a much bigger meal for you."

So the troll let Little Billy Goat Gruff cross the bridge to the other side. Then the troll patiently waited for Middle Billy Goat Gruff to come trip-trapping across the bridge. The troll was quite hungry, but decided he could wait for the middle goat.

In a little while, Middle Billy Goat Gruff started across the wooden bridge.

Trip-trap, trip-trap, trip-trap, went Middle Billy Goat Gruff.

"Who's that trip-trapping across my bridge?" roared the troll.

"It is only I, Middle Billy Goat Gruff," he said.

"I'm coming to eat you up!" said the troll.

"Oh, no!" said Middle Billy Goat Gruff loudly. "I am only a middle-sized billy goat. Wait for my brother, Big Billy Goat Gruff. He will make a much bigger dinner for you to eat."

The troll let Middle Billy Goat Gruff across the bridge.

Finally Big Billy Goat Gruff crossed the bridge.

TRIP-TRAP, TRIP-TRAP, TRIP-TRAP, went Big Billy Goat Gruff as he walked on the bridge.

"Who's TRIP-TRAPPING across my bridge?" roared the troll.

"It is I, Big Billy Goat Gruff," he said.

"I'm coming to eat you up!" said the troll. The troll climbed onto the bridge. Then Big Billy Goat Gruff, with his two big horns, tossed the troll high into the air, and he fell down into the river below.

The troll was gone! All the animals were free to cross the bridge without fear.

The three Billy Goats Gruff were happy to be on the other side. They feasted on the green grass and wildflowers.

"I was right," said Little Billy Goat Gruff. "The grass tastes as sweet as it smells."

"And I was right, too," said Middle Billy Goat Gruff. "The flowers taste like honey."

"Best of all, I was right," said Big Billy Goat Gruff. "We were able to trick the evil troll and cross the bridge."

So the three Billy Goats Gruff spent their summer happily eating in the high meadows. They grew very fat and contented.

Instead of playing hide-and-seek amongst the rocks, the three Billy Goats Gruff could run and jump and play tag in the open field. And Big Billy Goat Gruff did not always have to be "It." But because he was bigger and a little slower than all the other animals, Big Billy Goat Gruff was "It" many times anyway. But that was just fine. The three Billy Goats Gruff had fun playing on the other side of the river.

Soon the weather began to grow cold again. It was autumn and the three happy Billy Goats Gruff came down from the high meadows.

This time they crossed over the bridge without a worry. After Big Billy Goat Gruff tossed him into the river, the wicked troll was never seen again.

From then on, the billy goats spent every winter along the rocky mountainside and each summer prancing in the grassy meadow. They never had to worry about the evil troll.

The other animals were also very happy not to have to worry about the troll. Everyone was free to cross the bridge from one side of the river to the other.

But whether they were playing hide-and-seek amongst the rocks or tag in the meadow, no billy goat was able to cross to the other side of the river for a hiding place or to get away from being tagged. It was a rule they had to make, since now they were free to cross the river any time they wanted.

Zoo Fun

Written by Sarah Toast
Illustrated by Joe Veno

Mark and Mindy like being next-door neighbors. But there is something even better than being each other's neighbor: They are neighbors to the city zoo!

Mark and Mindy visit the zoo a lot. This morning, they decide to play a little game as they walk through the zoo.

"Look at the neat animals on the gate!" says Mindy, as they go through the entrance gate.

"We should try to visit all of these animals today," says Mark.

"It looks like the elephant and the giraffe are waiting for us," says Mindy. "Let's go see them first."

The huge elephant is taking its morning shower from its long, strong trunk while a tiny bird sits on its back. The elephant is the biggest land animal on earth, but it only eats plants.

"I'd like to have a trunk to pick up really big and heavy things," says Mark.

"I'd like to water the garden with my trunk," says Mindy.

Mark and Mindy take turns pretending that they are great big elephants. They use their arms for trunks and swing them back and forth lazily.

Mark tries to make an elephant noise.

"You sound like a trumpet!" laughs Mindy.

"That's what elephants sound like," says Mark.

Just then the elephant trumpets loudly. Mark and Mindy cover their ears.

"Wow! I guess you're right," says Mindy. "You make a good elephant sound."

"It would be fun to be an elephant. You would be so big that nobody could bother you," says Mark. "And I really like peanuts, too." He laughs as he waves his trunk.

The long-necked giraffe can be seen above the treetops. Mark and Mindy stroll over for a closer look.

The giraffe is the tall, silent type, steadily munching on the tender leaves at the tips of the topmost branches.

Mark and Mindy stretch themselves as tall as they can. They agree that they would like to be as tall as a giraffe so that they could see for miles.

"We would never lose sight of our car in the parking lot," says Mindy. "My mom doesn't like that."

"Yeah. And we would always have the best seats whenever we go to the movies," says Mark.

When the giraffe stretches his long neck to reach some tasty leaves next to Mark and Mindy, they see that the giraffe has a purple tongue.

"Wow! I think that giraffe has been eating a grape popsicle," says Mindy, laughing.

Mark and Mindy stick out their tongues to see if their tongues are purple, too. They walk around the zoo stretching tall and poking out their tongues. It is a silly sight!

"Roar! Roar!" Mark and Mindy hear the lion's thunderous roar and run to find it. They see a big, powerful lion roaring at the crowd as he walks back and forth.

The shaggy-maned male lions roar the most, but the female lions are the ones that hunt for most of the lion family's food.

Mark and Mindy pretend to roar like big lions. They hold out their fingers to pretend they are claws.

"Do you know that a lion family is called a pride?" says Mindy.

"Yes. I wonder if that means they are very proud animals," says Mark. He scratches his head.

"Sometimes my cat at home looks like a lion," says Mindy.

"It's a good thing you don't have a real lion at home because you would have to feed it antelope and wildebeest and things like that," says Mark.

"Ew," says Mindy. "I'm glad my cat likes cat food."

Mark and Mindy pretend to be lions again. They roar at each other. Then they roar at the lion.

"I'm scarier than you are," says Mindy.

"No, I'm scarier," says Mark.

Mark and Mindy hear the chattering of lively monkeys and dash over to watch them. The monkeys swing between branches, holding on with their hands and feet. They use their long, strong grasping tails mostly for balance. When they want to, monkeys can move fast through the trees.

Mark and Mindy would like to have fun all day like the monkeys. Mark says, "I'd eat bananas for breakfast, lunch, and dinner."

Mindy says, "I'd never walk on the ground. I'd swing from tree to tree."

"What would you do when you run out of trees?" asks Mark.

"Then I'd jump on your head and let you carry me around," laughs Mindy. Mark laughs, too.

Then Mark and Mindy run around the zoo making monkey noises. They pretend to eat bananas.

"Do banana splits count?" asks Mark.

Mindy just laughs and jumps on a park bench making monkey sounds. Mark jumps on the bench, too.

"We are very silly monkeys," says Mindy.

Next, the two friends visit the bottle-nosed dolphins swimming in their pool. The playful dolphins are a small type of whale. The dolphins swim fast to catch fish, but they also swim just for fun.

"If we could swim underwater like that, then we could swim around the world through all the oceans," says Mark, as he and Mindy pretend to swim as fast as dolphins.

Mindy makes chattering noises like the dolphins. She pretends that she is balancing on her powerful back tail.

Suddenly Mark and Mindy catch sight of a herd of gazelles leaping gracefully in a grassy field. The two friends bound over to watch the swift-footed gazelles speeding along.

"I'd like to run so fast that I seem to fly," says Mark.

"And I'd like to leap high and far," says Mindy. "Boy, we could really go places!"

Mark and Mindy run like gazelles. They run as fast as they can, then leap through the air.

"I feel like a ballet dancer," says Mindy.

The two run and laugh until they almost fall down from exhaustion.

Soon, Mark and Mindy come to the penguins. Penguins are birds that don't fly, but they swim very well. The penguins like to belly flop on snow and ice, then dive into the cold water. When they swim, their wings are like flippers, and they steer with their webbed feet.

"I'd like to have that much fun in cold weather," says Mark.

"I'm not sure I could swim in such cold water, though," says Mindy. "I would be blue, not black and white."

"The penguins look like they are dressed for a fancy party," says Mark, pretending to straighten his imaginary bow tie.

Mark and Mindy waddle and toddle like the penguins on the ice. They pretend that they are at a fancy party, too.

"How do you do?" asks Mindy.

"Quite well, thank you," says Mark.

The two laugh as they waddle around the penguin exhibit. Being a penguin is fun, they think.

"It is starting to get a little late," says Mindy.

"Come on! We have one more animal to visit today," says Mindy. They stop waddling and run out of the penguin house.

Next Mark and Mindy go inside the darkened bat house. When their eyes get used to the darkness, Mark and Mindy can see dozens of bats swooping around the room.

Bats aren't birds, but they have large wings and fly at night. By listening to echoes of their own squeaks, bats can find insects to eat. They are very useful because they like to eat mosquitoes.

Mark and Mindy pretend they have wings. "I'd like to swoop through the air like a bat," says Mark.

"But would you like to sleep all day and eat bugs at night?" asks Mindy.

Mark makes a face and continues to fly around. Sleeping all day would be no fun, he thinks. He would be awake when all his friends were asleep. Mark doesn't like this idea.

Now it really is getting late, and Mark and Mindy must leave the zoo. They buy a few colorful balloons on their way out.

"We did it!" says Mindy as they leave through the zoo gate. "Let's play the animal game again tomorrow."

Little Ant Goes to School

Written by Brian Conway
Illustrated by Richard Bernal

L ittle Andy Ant used to spend each day with his pull toy, happily playing outside in the warm summer sun. Then, as the summer days got shorter, the sun didn't feel so warm anymore.

"Summer is over," Andy's mother told him. "That means today is your first day of school!"

Andy had heard about school. He didn't want to be cooped up inside all day long.

School was a strange, new place. Little Andy Ant wasn't ready to go. He was scared and a little sad.

"Can I take my toy along with me?" Andy asked.

"School is for children," his mother answered, "not for toys."

Little Andy Ant tried to be brave. His mother walked him to school that day.

"Maybe school won't be so bad," she said, "once you give it a try." So Andy agreed to try school for just one day.

At school Andy had his very own desk. And he had never seen so many busy little ants bustling around in one place!

Teacher gave the children lots of things to do. Everybody got their own paper and pens! Then they learned all about reading and writing.

"You know how ants work together to make anthills?" Andy asked Teacher. "I think letters work together the same way to make words."

Teacher said Andy was right! He was pretty good at drawing and painting and numbers, too!

Little Andy Ant strolled home from school after a long day. Learning new things was fun, and reading and writing were pretty cool, too.

"Maybe you were right," little Andy Ant told his mother. "Maybe school's not so bad after all."

Andy decided to try school for one more day. The morning passed by quickly for him. Before Andy knew it, it was already lunchtime!

Andy followed the other children to the lunchroom. They got pretty wild there, so Andy sat away from all the noise.

Then Lunch Lady called out, "Cookies and milk!"

What a commotion that caused! Little Andy Ant squeezed his way through and got one tiny chunk of cookie. Then he knew what all the fuss was about. Lunch Lady made the best cookies Andy had ever tasted!

Andy trotted home from school. Lunchtime was a pleasant break, and Lunch Lady's cookies were especially good!

"Maybe you were right, Mom," said little Andy Ant. "Maybe school's not so bad after all."

Andy thought he'd try school for another day. As soon as Andy got there, Teacher said they were going to the woods for an all-day field trip.

Andy learned about new plants and berries at every turn!

Some older children made a campfire with their teacher. They needed Andy's help.

"I know how to find the best twigs!" Andy said. He whistled for his friend Tweeter Bird.

Tweeter Bird brought back the finest twigs in the woods. There were enough twigs to build a campfire and for each little ant to roast a marshmallow. All the children at school liked Andy and his friend Tweeter very much.

Andy happily hopped home from school that day. He not only had his own desk, but there were field trips and recess, too!

"Maybe you were right, Mom," said little Andy Ant. "Maybe school's not so bad after all."

The next day, Andy wanted to try school again. He didn't know what to expect in school that day, but he had an idea it might be fun.

"I wonder what will happen today," Andy said to himself.

Little Andy Ant sat down at his desk. One of the children whispered, "Please come to my birthday party today."

Andy ran home that day. Up until then, Andy thought that birthdays only happened once a year. Now he learned that he could celebrate his birthday *and* his friends' birthdays, too!

"I think you were right, Mom," said little Andy Ant. "Maybe school's not so bad after all."

Andy had fun at his school friend's party. He ate some delicious birthday cake and even got seconds!

Little Andy Ant couldn't wait to get to school the next day! He hoped it was somebody else's birthday. And he wanted to learn how to count up to really big numbers, like how many birthdays his class would have.

Andy made up a new outside game for his friends that day at recess. Everybody loved to swing and dive! They looked up to Andy as the most adventurous ant in their class.

"You're the best, Andy!" the children shouted.

Little Andy Ant rushed home from school after another fun day. He was so excited!

Birthday Cake Mix-Up

Written by Lisa Harkrader
Illustrated by Sherry Neidigh

Barry Bumblebee sat straight up in bed. He rubbed his eyes and looked out the window.

"Oh, no!" cried Barry. "The sun is up. I'm late."

Barry had to go to work before most bugs in town were even awake. He was the owner of the Busy Bee Bakery. The bakery made the most delicious baked goods in town. Barry pulled on his white apron and baker's hat. Then he rushed out the door.

When Barry arrived at the bakery, his helpers were already busy. Two bees sifted flour while another bee measured cinnamon for a batch of sticky buns.

Three other bees mixed batter for the blueberry muffins.

"We have cherry popovers in the oven, and pumpernickel rolls cooling on a rack. The only things left to make are raisin bread and chocolate chip cookies," said Barry. "I'll make those myself."

He reached in his pocket for his glasses. But they weren't there. "Oh, no!" cried Barry. "Now where did I leave my glasses?"

Barry squinted at the clock. The bakery would be opening soon. There was no time to look for his glasses!

"I bake raisin bread and chocolate chip cookies every day," said Barry. "I don't need my glasses."

Barry set out two mixing bowls. He measured the ingredients for cookies with one hand and mixed bread batter with another. He pulled out a box of raisins and a bag of chocolate chips from the cupboard. Barry busily poured the raisins into one bowl and the chocolate chips into the other. When Barry finished making the cookies and the bread, he put them into the oven.

Soon the oven timer dinged. Barry squinted at the clock.

"Time to take my goodies from the oven and open the Busy Bee Bakery," he said.

Carla and Casey Cricket were the first to arrive at the bakery.

"You're just in time to taste some freshly baked treats," Barry said. He gave Carla a slice of bread and handed Casey a cookie.

"I love raisin cookies," said Casey.

"Yum," said Carla. "I've never had chocolate chip bread before."

"Oh, no! I mixed up the ingredients," cried Barry.

"Don't worry," said Carla. "These are delicious treats!"

"Thank you," said Barry. "Now I need to bake a birthday cake for my niece Bibi."

Barry pulled out his cookbook. He squinted at Bibi's favorite cake recipe. "A crate of flour," he read. "A whole crate?" Barry dumped a crate of flour into his biggest mixing bowl. "Two dozen eggs," Barry read. Barry cracked two dozen eggs, and mixed them into the flour. He added the rest of the ingredients and poured the batter into his biggest pan. He set it in the oven.

When the timer dinged, Barry peeked into the oven. "Oh, no!" he cried. "This cake is huge!"

The other bees helped him pull the cake from the oven. It was the biggest cake any of them had ever seen!

"I wanted to make Bibi something wonderful and ended up making something terrible," moaned Barry. "I should've used two eggs, not two dozen. And a cup of flour, not a crate."

Barry squinted at the clock again. "I don't have time to bake another one," he said.

The bees frosted the cake, and set it on a cart. "It's not so bad," they told him. But Barry didn't believe them. He rolled the giant cake to Bibi's house anyway.

"I hope Bibi isn't too disappointed," he said to himself.

The party had already started. The guests took one look at the cake and gasped.

Barry shook his head. "Bibi, I'm sorry."

"For what?" Bibi gave her uncle a big hug. "This is the most wonderful birthday cake I've ever seen. Nobody else has ever had a cake so big. Uncle Barry, you're the greatest."

The other guests began to clap. Barry sighed with relief.

At the end of the party Bibi gave her uncle a surprise. "I found your glasses," she said. "I hope you didn't need them at work today."

THE
END